when
rivals *fall*

BAYSHORE RIVALS BOOK ONE

USA Today Bestselling Author

J. L. BECK
C. HALLMAN

J. L. Beck
xoxo

Welcome to Bayshore's
Cassy

PROLOGUE

2 Years Prior

"Take the baggie, and put it in Sullivan's pocket," My father orders, not even looking up from the papers sprawled across his desk.

In his pocket? No way in Hell do I want to get that close to that asshole. I'll try and get Shelby to help me with it. I'm not getting within ten feet of him or his brothers.

The Bishop Brothers, Sullivan, Oliver, and Banks are the children of Chloe and George Bishop, our rivals. They're disgustingly handsome, filthy rich, and manipulative liars. Every occurrence I've ever had with them was one that ended with me wanting to stab them in the eye with the nearest object.

I don't know exactly when or how it started, all I know is that the hate between our two families has been growing for the last two decades. Ever since I can remember I've been told about the Bishops and how they were trying to ruin our business, my family's livelihood.

Recently, we had to fire an entire crew right before Christmas. A dozen families out of a job before the holidays and all because of them.

Who does something that cruel? That's not the worst thing they've done either, but it is the icing on the cake. Lately, their antics have been affecting more than just my family. Their wrath rippling down the line and onto our workers. I don't bother to ask what the Bishops have done this time. It doesn't matter. We'll get even. We always do.

Sullivan the youngest of the Bishop Brothers is my age and even though we don't go to the same school, we do occasionally run into each other at events and parties.

Usually, I try to avoid him like the plague. But today I'm going to the same place as him and on purpose. Everyone from every high school across the county will be there no matter the last name.

Tightening my grip on my purse, I ask, "What's in the bag?"

"Don't ask questions you don't want answers to, Harlow. Put the bag in his pocket and I'll make sure the rest gets done," My father answers with a tone that tells me to shut my mouth and do as I'm told.

I bite my bottom lip, wondering if I should push the issue. I don't like the Bishops, in fact, I hate them for what they've done and how they've treated my family for the last couple of years but I'm getting tired of doing my parents bidding. Tired of the constant hate. I decide against making a scene, there's no point. I'll end up having to do it anyway.

"Should I come home right afterward?"

Looking up from the document in front of him he pierces me with a stare from his blue eyes that match my own in depth and color.

A sinister grin finds its way onto his lips. "No. I

want you to stick around. Make sure they see who it was that set them up."

"Got it." I nod and grab the baggie from the edge of the desk. The contents of the bag must be light because it feels like there isn't anything inside it.

"Don't forget all they've done to us, sweetie." My father's voice softens. "I wouldn't ask you to do these things if I didn't feel it was justified. I have to protect you, my businesses, my men and everything those filthy Bishops do is a direct attack against us."

"I know, Dad." My lips pull up into a reassuring smile. Even if I hate what I have to do, being a part of this rivalry, I know there isn't anything I can do to change it. My last name is Lockwood, and it will always be family over honor.

It's my job to protect my family's legacy.

"I'll get the job done," I mumble and turn on my heels exiting his office.

Once in the hall I pause and lean against the wall.

I can do this. I will do this.

I remind myself of how Chloe and George Bishop stare down at me like I'm gum stuck to the bottom of their shoes every time we cross paths. Their three sons are not much better. Annoyingly handsome and full of themselves. Sullivan is the worst. He acts like he is the king of the world and everyone is beneath him, like it's our duty to bow to him.

Tonight, we'll put an end to his reign.

Tonight, he'll find out what happens when you mess with a Lockwood.

CHAPTER ONE

Present

B ayshore University is not the prestigious college that I thought I would be attending. My whole life I thought I would end up going to one of the best Ivy League schools in the country, like Yale or Harvard, just like every other rich kid from my high school. Instead, I chose to attend this place. A nice but low-key University located on the west coast, hundreds of miles away from my hometown of North Woods. Most kids wouldn't choose to be miles away from their parents, but I wasn't most. I chose this college because it's as far away from my family as I can get.

As soon as I turned eighteen and I got my hands on my trust fund, I was out of my parents' house. There was no way I was going to stay another minute longer. I wanted to disappear, forget about my last name, and what it meant.

After finding out about the things my father had been up to, I didn't want a single thing to do with the family business.

"This is college, and you're acting as though someone has sentenced you to ten years hard labor." Shelby laughs. My nose wrinkles as I look up at the fortress before me. Of course, the place would look more like a medieval castle set in the Scottish Highlands than a university. Ropes of thick green ivy climb the walls like they're trying to escape.

"Maybe not ten years, but at least four, right?" I grin.

"College isn't a dick, Harlow. Stop making it so hard."

"Nice analogy. Where did you pull that one out of?"

"My ass." She grins and slams her hips into mine. I roll my eyes like I'm annoyed with her when in reality I'm grateful she is here. She really had to talk her parents into letting her attend college here. I think the only reason her dad agreed is because he's had a bad year at his law firm and the tuition is cheaper than Stanford, where Shelby was supposed to go originally. She doesn't seem to care though.

Students rush past us in a flurry to get into their dorm rooms, while Shelby and I take our sweet time. We had most of our things shipped to the college, all except our personal belongings so there's no rush for us. We spend most of our time taking in the surroundings. The University itself is beautiful, with huge oak trees, and sprawling areas of lush green grass, that I can picture myself sitting on with a blanket and a good book.

We make it to the crowded dorm and up the stairs to our room without incident. Once inside I exhale all the air from my lungs and sag down onto my small twin size bed. The dorms are small and leave very little room for privacy but that's okay. The place is close to the ocean and has a view that most would dream of.

"Okay, so I was invited to a party by a couple of guys I met over at Starbucks," Shelby says, tossing her blonde hair over her shoulder.

"We've been here less than twenty-four hours and you want to go to a party already?" I knew parties were going to happen, but I'd hoped to avoid them.

"It's a past time set forth by our ancestors, when you arrive at college you must party."

"Sounds like its set forth by Shelby." I roll my eyes.

Shelby juts out her bottom lip into a firm pout, "Oh, come on, Harlow, you only went to a handful of parties when we were in high school and now you don't want to enjoy college. Your parents are out of the picture, you can basically do anything you want."

She has no idea how wrong she is. Yes, I've managed to escape my father's clutches for now, but I'm not going to be able to hide from him and my mother forever.

"If I go will you at least wait a whole month before inviting me to another one?"

Amusement twinkles in Shelby's hazel eyes, "Mmm, two weeks tops."

"Seriously." I cringe.

"It's college, Harlow, and I'm your certified fun helper."

Shaking my head, I say, "You're not a fun helper, you're a get into trouble helper."

She taps at her chin with her finger, "Trouble. Fun. All sounds the same to me. Now, what are you wearing? Better be something sexy. We've got to grab the boys' attention right off the bat. You know college boys, all ADHD squirrel like."

"I'm not catching anything, and especially not any

boys' attention."

I'd garnered enough attention from the Bishop Brothers back home. After what I did to Sullivan, I was surprised he could walk past me without wanting to murder me. Let's just say it made social gatherings a little tense.

"Your parents aren't here. You don't have anything to worry about. You're free." Shelby gets up from her bed and puts her arms out like a bird, flapping them until she reaches my bed, slamming herself down onto it, causing me to bounce and a bubble of laughter to escape my throat.

"I'm not worried about them," I lie. I'm worried about them just as much as I'm worried about the Bishops.

Actually, I'm not worried. I'm terrified. For years I've helped my father spread rumors about the Bishops. I've helped ruin their lives and for what? Nothing, it was all for nothing. I didn't know how horrible my father really was. He didn't just want their business, he wanted them gone.

At one point my hate for the Bishops started to diminish, and in its place resentment towards my father bloomed. I didn't want anything to do with my old life, the drama, the hate, the revenge. I wanted to forget that part of my life ever existed.

"Good, because it wouldn't matter if you were. Now, up. Let me see what I have to work with and then what clothing you've brought with you."

"Do we really have to go?" I bat my long eyelashes knowing damn well it won't work. I can't make myself look as innocent and sweet as Shelby does. Plus, I kind of owe it to her to at least go out once. She did, after all, move hundreds of miles away from her family to be a supportive friend.

"Yes." She smiles and I should've known that smile was going to be the death of me.

I pull on the bottom of the miniskirt that Shelby shoved me into. I'm not exactly skinny, curvy is more like it, and even though I don't have any real self-confidence issues, this thing is so short every single guy here is going to get a flash of my crotch by the end of the night.

If and that's a pretty big *if* I go out with Shelby again, she will not be dressing me.

Brushing a few strands of my silky blonde hair behind my ear I survey the crowded room. The frat house is filled to max occupancy with women and men of all ages. There's dancing, singing, and drinking games. People chilling on the couch in the living room, smoking what I'm pretty sure isn't cigarettes based on the sweet aroma that permeates the air.

"We made it." Shelby huffs, a wide grin on her blood red painted lips. She acts like she just aced a test that she's been studying for all semester. We stand together, side by side, in the middle of the room, watching as people move around it, chatting, and having the time of their lives. The longer we stand there the more attention we bring to ourselves.

I can feel eyes on me, gliding over my bare legs, and my shirt that hangs off of one shoulder. Yeah, I don't like this. Being the center of attention. Feeling out of place and a little timid, I hide behind the curtain of my hair as I turn to Shelby.

"We came, we saw, we had some fun, can we go now?" I whine, tugging on her arm. I haven't been to a party since that night. *That disastrous night.* A shiver runs down my spine at the memory, at the anger, and simmering rage that reflected back at me from all three of the Bishop Brothers.

"We'll make you pay for this, Harlow. One day you won't have your parents' protection, and then what will you do?"

Shrugging I say, "I'm not scared of you. You're weak. Pathetic. Just like your parents."

Oliver entered my bubble of space, forcing me to take a step back or be chest to chest with him, "One day, we'll get even with you. We'll break you. You'll wish you were never born."

"You'll be waiting a long time..." I sneer, feeling the fear slither up my spine and around my throat like a snake.

Wiggling my shoulders, I shake off the unpleasant emotions coming with the memory.

"Nope." Shelby pops the p, and grabs onto my hand, tugging us deeper into the house. The place is huge, similar to the mansion I lived in back home. There are priceless paintings on the walls, crown molding, and chandeliers that cost more than most cars. It reminds me so much of my old life that I have to shake away the creepy feeling slithering up my back. I did my research when selecting a college and I made certain this one wouldn't have any billionaire co-eds.

As far as I know, Shelby and I are the only two people attending this university with parents that make more than a million a year. Which leaves me to wonder whose house it is? Does another student own it? His or her parents? *Why do you even care, Harlow?*

Paranoid. I'm being paranoid. Ever since leaving

North Woods I've wondered when my past would come back to haunt me. All the things I said and did. The guilt eats away at me every single day. I let my father lead me blindly into the dark. I let him feed me lie after lie. I thought I was doing the right thing, but I wasn't.

When we enter the kitchen I notice the black marble counters and stainless steel appliances. Off the kitchen is a pair of patio doors that open up to a backyard that butts up to the beach. It's beautiful really, minus all the college coeds that are liquored up.

There's a makeshift bar set up on the huge island and Shelby gets to work mixing us something to drink. *Everything's okay.* I tell myself, blowing out air through my mouth, before inhaling through my nose.

"Here," Shelby says, her pink painted nails coming into view as she shoves a red cup into my hand, the contents sloshing against the sides of the cup. I peer inside of it before bringing it to my nose to sniff.

"What is this? It smells like straight alcohol."

Shelby shrugs, her hazel eyes narrowing, "Just drink it. Live a little, will you? If you promise to have a good time, I'll promise not to push you to go out with me so much. Deal?"

Ugh, as much as I hate to admit it, she's right. I'm eighteen, a college student. I need to live a little, and enjoy the years ahead of me before they're gone and I'm forced to be an actual adult, with a job, and responsibilities.

"Fine. I'll try." I give her a weak smile and take a drink of the pink looking liquid. The burn I was expecting doesn't come and I'm pleasantly surprised by the cherry tang that's left against my lips.

"Good, huh?" Shelby asks, watching me like a

hawk.

"Decent. It doesn't taste like I'm drinking lighter fluid."

"Shut up." She giggles, taking a drink from her cup. The hairs on the back of my neck stand on end and I don't understand why. Swinging my gaze around the room I look for anything out of place. *What's wrong with me? I think I'm losing my mind.*

A loud rap song comes blaring through the speakers, vibrating through the masses of bodies and into my skull, causing a dull ache to form there. A book wouldn't give me this kind of headache. Feeling as if I'll need it, I drink the rest of the liquid in my cup and hand it back to Shelby with a mischievous grin.

"Make me another. I'm going to go find a bathroom. If I'm not back in ten minutes send out a search party."

"Don't be so dramatic." She takes the cup and ushers me away. "Go to the bathroom. I'll be here when you get back."

Leaving the kitchen I notice a group of women in skirts shorter than my own enter the house. My heart sinks into my stomach at the sight. *Barbies.* Three girls dolled up like plastic dolls. Fake. Popular. Gorgeous. Every college and high school has them.

They stick out like a weed in a bed of flowers. They giggle, and toss their hair over their shoulders, batting their eyelashes at every man that looks their way, and there are a lot of men looking their way. Turning, I head for the huge staircase before they come any closer, I know their type—they'll either want to befriend me and initiate me into their clan, or they'll make me public enemy number one—I don't want to get on their radar, I want to have an uneventful, low-key college experience.

Rushing up the stairs I almost run head first into a couple that is making out against the railing.

I mumble a half-hearted apology and continue in search of a bathroom. I open one door to find an empty bedroom with a large inviting looking bed in the center. How bad is it that I would rather curl up in that bed and read a book than go back downstairs and party with the other students?

When I pull the door shut behind me, a familiar scent coming from inside the room tickles my nose. I can't quite place the unique smell, something like a forest after a rainy day.

I keep walking down the hall and the next door I open is actually a bathroom. I disappear inside, locking the door behind me. It is almost as big as my dorm room. I shake my head at the size and fanciness of it all.

I use to think this is all that mattered, money, pretty things and people who look up to you. That's what my family taught me to think and there was a time when I didn't question anything my parents told me. That time is over. Now I know better.

I'm still thinking about the familiar scent in that bedroom as I wash my hands. Something about it is nagging me but I just can't put my finger on it. Looking in the mirror, I give myself a once over before exiting the bathroom. I really should act more like the other people around here. Have fun and enjoy college life. This is what I wanted. I got away from my family to be normal. All I have to do now is get out of my own head and enjoy this.

I walk back down the hall, forcing myself not to think about the bedroom with its tempting scent. I fight the urge to take another peek inside. Just as I pass it I hear the soft click of a door opening, but before I have the time to truly comprehend that someone is behind me, I'm grabbed by my arm and yanked into the room.

Screaming like someone is about to kill me I stumble into the room, losing my footing as I go. Arms flailing, I prepare myself to land hard on the ground but I'm shocked when a pair of strong arms circle my waist from behind pulling me flush to a firm, warm chest.

Momentarily I'm stunned, like a doe caught in the headlights of a car. My screams cut off, the air stills in my lungs. I can't do anything. I'm frozen in place. *What's happening?*

All I can hear is the swooshing of blood in my ears, my chest heaving up and down with panic. I open my mouth to scream again, but nothing comes out. Suddenly I'm dizzy, the smell of rain fills my nostrils once more and I realize immediately who that scent belongs to.

"Did you miss me? Is that why you're here, in my bedroom? Eager to see what we have in store for you?" Sullivan's dark voice fills the room, and a cold shiver runs through me. I notice then that he's standing a few feet away from me, but his voice affects me as if he is right beside me whispering in my ear. It doesn't matter that I can't fully see him. I don't need to. I know he's looking at me with disgust.

His room? Blinking slowly, I try to digest what he's just said? Confused I'm about to ask him what the hell he is talking about when I realize someone is still holding on to my waist. Their warm hands burning into my skin.

Spinning around I shove at the firm chest in front of me, realizing quickly its Banks, the middle Bishop brother. A sinister grin spreads across his face as he licks his lips. "I think she just missed us, why else would she come here, to our house?"

"Your house?" I finally find my voice again. It's shaky but at least I got the words out.

"Yes, *our* house." A third voice drawls, and my gaze travels across the room and collides with Oliver's chocolate brown eyes. "We bought it recently, figured it would be nicer than living in the dorms."

Dorms? Why would they be living in the dorms?

Nothing makes sense right now. This has to be a dream, no scratch that, this is a freaking nightmare. I shake my head as if I can wake myself up from it. Then I try and take a step towards the door, but Sullivan slaps a hand over the handle halting my movement.

"Not so fast," he growls, his muscled form towering over me. He's bigger than he was the last time I saw him. Taller, scarier, even more disgustingly handsome than I remember. "Let's talk. We want to tell you how this year is going to go."

What does he mean? How this year is going to go? He can't really be saying what I think he is? The Bishop brothers aren't... they can't be... My chest starts to heave, even though no air is filling my lungs. Lord, please tell me they aren't attending college here.

"I don't think she gets it," Banks taunts, devilishly.

"It's not hard to figure out. I mean, we're laying it out pretty clearly. It's a shame really. All that money and her daddy couldn't even get her a proper education." Oliver sneers.

"I'm not stupid." I try and make the words sound strong, but they come out like a soft breeze whispering through the trees.

"Right, you're only a liar," Oliver responds, his words like a slap to the face.

Gritting my teeth, I let the insult sink in. *He's not wrong, I am a liar.* Because of my father I've done a lot of things I'm not proud of. I followed him like a lamb to the slaughter, believing him with blind faith. I knew someday karma would catch up with me. That eventually, I would pay for my wrongdoings, I just never expected it to be so soon.

"Let me put it into words even someone like you can understand," Sullivan leans in so closely, I can feel the heat of his body. I can feel all three of them, their bodies drawn to mine like a magnet.

"Remember when I told you I would make you pay for what you did that night?"

Saliva sticks to the inside of my throat—like honey —making it hard to swallow. Every nightmare I've had over the last year would never have amounted to this. All three of their faces have haunted me in my sleep since that night. I regretted doing it as soon as I did it, but there was no taking it back, there was no changing the course we were headed on. It was like a bad accident, that you couldn't look away from.

As if he can see the worry filling my features his smile widens, perfectly straight white teeth gleam in the moonlight filtering in through the window blinds.

"That little stunt ruined his senior year. Got him suspended from the team. You tarnished our family name, but that was the point, right?" Oliver hisses, his eyes narrowing, his angular jaw—sharp enough to cut glass—clenching.

The Bishops' had money, but nothing could stop the local papers from printing an article about their son doing drugs and getting booted from the team. My father had hit his mark and made them bleed, and worse he'd used me to do it.

"Well, now that our family business is ruined, there is nothing for us to take over, so I guess we all have to go to college after all," Banks explains, and I finally get it. All three of them will be attending Bayshore. *This can't be happening.*

"Please... look...." An apology is sitting on the edge of my tongue, but a hand comes out of nowhere from behind me and presses against my mouth—another at my hip—effectively cutting off the words before I get a chance to say them.

I know who it is that has ahold of me, and I try to wiggle out of Banks' hold, but he just pulls me closer, until my back is pressed firmly into his muscular chest. Panic, and something else, something warm, and euphoric swirl in my belly.

No. I won't be attracted to them, and their stupid muscles, hard abs, and devilish smiles. They're the enemy, my rivals.

"Shh, Princess. We didn't say you could speak. Keep your mouth shut, otherwise, we'll find a better use for it." Banks' smooth voice tickles my ear as he pulls his hand away from my mouth. His body remains close to mine, too close, but for some reason, I don't move right away. One of his hands remains on my hip and I just stand there for a moment, letting his body heat seep into me, trying to warm the icy cold blood running through my veins.

"I told you... I promised you, that you would pay, and now it's time. It's time to pay your dues." Tears sting my eyes. *Don't cry. Don't cry.* I will not cry in front of them. I won't.

Finding a sliver of strength, I jab my elbow into

Banks' ribs. He releases me, even though I know I didn't hit him hard enough to hurt.

"Is that all you've got?" he snickers.

I step toward the door that Sullivan is now blocking with his body.

"Let me go," I grit out through my teeth.

No one moves, or says a single word, it's almost like they're waiting for Sullivan to make a choice and that terrifies me. After a long second, he finally moves out of the way, a smug grin painted on his face. Waving his hand over the door and motioning me to leave, he says, "You may leave tonight, but you can never get away from us. We'll find you wherever you go, and we *will* make you pay for what you did."

CHAPTER TWO

Running down the stairs as fast as I can, I almost trip, missing the last step. I can't form a single thought besides the one telling me that I need to get out of here. Scanning the crowded room I look for Shelby. She isn't anywhere to be found and I grow increasingly worried with each second that passes.

I can't breathe. I need to go, get as far away from this place as I can. My feet start to move on their own, and I find I'm moving through the crowd of people, pushing some out of the way as I go. Before I know it I've made it to the front door. I suck in a greedy breath of fresh air, my heart racing so fast inside my chest that it feels like I'm having a heart attack.

What the hell just happened?

Reaching into my back pocket I pull out my phone so I can send Shelby a text telling her that I'm outside and ready to go. She appears in the front yard a minute later shaking her head at me.

"What the hell, Harlow? We just got here," when she sees my face her expression sobers. "What's wrong? Did something happen? You look like you've seen a ghost."

"Do you know who owns this house? Who invited you to this party?" As soon as I ask the question her lips curl into a deep frown.

"Well, I didn't at first but I kind of figured it out. I didn't think it was going to be that big of a deal. They just want to be friends. Is that really so bad?" *She doesn't have the first clue what she's talking about.*

"You told them I was going to school here? When? How? And *why*?" I yell, threading my fingers through my long blonde hair. The rational part of me knows it's not her fault. She doesn't know about all of the things that have happened between the Bishops and my family, no one does besides the people involved.

My father made sure of it. He kept our name out of the whole incident not wanting to be tarnished and the Bishops didn't dare accuse me of planting the bag even though they knew it was me. Still, at this moment, I can't help but release my anger on her.

Her hazel—more green than brown in this light— eyes go wide, and she holds a hand to her chest.

"You're supposed to be my friend. How could you do this to me?" Shock and confusion are written all over my best friend's face as I scream the words at her. She has no idea what she's done wrong, and truthfully, I can't blame her.

Right now, I just need to leave. To get away.

Turning around I start to walk away from her, the house, and most importantly away from the Bishops. Everything is ruined now. They've come for their revenge and there isn't a damn thing I can do to stop them. I have no one to protect me now. After all I did for my father, I have no one to blame but myself. I'm the one who needs to suffer the consequences. Tears start to fall and I

swipe at them with the back of my hand. I knew coming
to this party was a mistake.

"Harlow," Shelby calls after me once, but I continue walking not paying her an ounce of attention. I'll
have to apologize later, but right now, I just can't deal
with it. Walking down the long driveway I kick at the
dirt. Stupid. I was so stupid to think that I could move
away, and that my problems would never find me. A
slight breeze blows off the ocean and whips my hair in
a million different directions, chilling me to the bone.
Wrapping my arms around myself I try and forget about
all that's lead me here.

All the mistakes I've made, the things I've done. I
don't know how long I walk but eventually, I reach the
end of the long driveway, just as a car is pulling into it. I
don't look up from the ground and hope that the car will
continue driving but I'm shocked when it comes to a halt
a few feet from me.

To make matters worse the driver's side window
rolls down a moment later.

"Hey, you okay? Do you need a ride?" I look up to
find a girl around the same age as me peering out the window, a smile on her lips. When she sees my face her smile
turns into a frown.

Do I look that bad?

"I don't know," I say more to myself than her.
Really, I don't know. I thought coming here would save
me, but it seems, it has only trapped me further.

"Come on, let me take you wherever it is that
you're walking." I should say no, should just keep walking. I don't know this girl. She could be a serial killer for
all I know. But her offer is tempting, and I don't want to
overthink it. I'll take my chances of being kidnapped or

killed over staying here.

"Sure. I just need a ride to the dorms," I tell her, walking over to the passenger side. She's driving an older jeep, something that, in my old town, no one would be caught driving.

Opening the door I climb in, the small overhead light turning on, casting a yellow glow over both of us. I pull the door shut behind me and grab the seat belt clicking it into place.

"I'm Caroline." She offers, as I get in the car and click the seat belt into place. She gives me another harmless smile that I can only make out because of the giant moon hanging in the sky.

Turning in my seat I take her in. She's young, like me, with short brown hair, she almost reminds me of a brunette tinker bell.

"Harlow," I say, trying to hide the sadness from my voice.

"Well, Harlow, you look like you could really use a drink. Everything okay?"

"Yeah, I'm fine. Just ran into some people from high school. Things didn't end well between me and those people so…" I trail off, staring out of the window.

"Ah, I get it. An old high school flame? Did you see him with another chick?" I almost laugh at her words. I wish it was that simple.

"No nothing like that. It's complicated," I sigh.

"If you want to talk about it I'm a great listener. Hey, which dorms are you in, you never said?"

"South wing, freshmen dorms," I mumble absentmindedly.

"I'm a freshman too. I live in the dorms across the street from you. I don't really know anybody here yet, so seriously if you ever want to hang out, I'm your girl. No pressure though."

"Thank you, I'll keep that in mind," I say when we pull up into the dorms parking lot. "Really, thanks, I appreciate it, and for the ride too."

"No problem. I'll see you around, Harlow," I give her a half-hearted wave and walk towards the entrance of the dorm. My mind is so consumed by my encounter with the Bishop Brothers that I don't realize how weird my encounter with Caroline was. I didn't even ask her why she was so late for the party, or why she was quick to bring me home when she hadn't even stepped foot in the party herself? Does she always pick up random people?

I shove my thoughts about her to the back of my mind and decide to digest them another day. Right now, I have to figure out how I'm going to remain going to school here with those assholes. When I get back to my room, I change into a pair of sleep pants, and an oversized T-shirt. I rid my face of the makeup painted on it, and sag down onto the small twin sized bed.

Tears sting my eyes once again and this time I let them fall. They cascade down my cheeks gently. I'm such a horrible friend. In my fit of panic and rage, I lashed out at the one and only friend I have here. I left her at that party without even thinking. Balling my hands into tiny fists I slam them against the blue comforter. I let those stupid assholes win by leaving, by running away. I want to scream. I've never been the type to run, to hide, but I don't want to fight them. I'm done fighting, done with the lies, with all the drama.

My eyes drift closed and I beg for sleep to come. Instead, images of the brothers filter through my mind. Tall, tan, handsome as hell. It would be so much easier to hate them if they weren't gorgeous and if the things my father had told me were true.

The memory of that night, haunts me, looming over me like a ghost. It's one of the worst and also, one of the best nights of my life all wrapped up in one.

The worst because I ruined the Bishops.

The best because I got my first kiss, even though it was with Sullivan Bishop.

I don't know how I'm going to get close to him. Bethany Kingston's house is packed making it hard to work my way through the crowd, and it doesn't help that I have no idea where he is. Parties aren't my scene and I'm sure I'm drawing attention to myself since I keep stopping and scanning the room, especially since I don't have a drink in my hand. A knot of worry fills my belly. I want to be at home, not out doing my father's dirty work.

The packet feels heavy in my pocket even though it's as light as a feather. All you have to do is put it in his pocket, I tell myself, surveying the room once more for his russet brown hair. The Bishop Brothers stand out amongst the other guys, not just because of their looks but because of the air that surrounds them. They walk with a chip on their shoulders, one that says I'm better than you.

"Come out to play, Princess?" A deep voice says from behind me, vibrating through me, and sending tiny rivulets of heat to my core. I shouldn't be attracted to them, but much like the rest of the female population I am and I hated myself for it.

"Not with you," I sneer, twisting around, coming face to face with Sullivan. Eyes as blue as the sky peer down at me. They're framed by thick lashes that most of the women at my school would die for. I clench my teeth together as I let my gaze roam over his face. High cheekbones, dimples, and full

smooth pink lips.

Him, Oliver, and Banks look almost identical, though Oliver has brown eyes that remind me of melted chocolate rather than blue like Banks and Sullivan. They are close in age, Oliver is two years older than us, Banks only a year.

Sullivan's pink lips turn into a pout, "That's a shame. I wonder what it is you do for fun? I never see you at parties like this."

"I don't like the people going to parties like this," I lie. I like most of the people here. I just don't like how people act at parties. I don't like the drinking or the dancing.

"If you don't like the crowd why don't we go out for a walk? Did you see the Kingston's' backyard yet?" I've heard about the backyard. It's supposed to be beautiful. Apparently, Mr. Kingston spends thousands of dollars every few weeks to have the most pristine yard with some of the rarest flowers. But going outside with Sullivan...just the two of us?

"Come on, I won't bite." He winks, giving me a swoon-worthy smile.

"Okay," I say, only partly so I get the chance to plant the baggy. He holds out his elbow and I hook my arm into his as we walk outside together. Stupidly the baggy is in the pocket I can't access with my arm intertwined with his like this.

It's very hard to see him as the bad guy when he is acting so nice to me. I have to remind myself about what his family has done to mine and stop thinking about how lovely it feels to walk so close to him.

As promised, he takes me on a walk, showing me the beautiful garden. We talk about school and the upcoming summer break as we admire the beauty of the unique flowers and warm light coming from the night sky. I hate to admit it to myself, but I'm actually having a good time. Why is he being so nice to me?

Doubt creeps up my spine and settles in the nape of my neck, giving me a subtle headache. I don't think I can do this. Maybe I just go back home and tell my dad I couldn't get to him.

"You okay?" Sullivan suddenly stops.

"Yes, sorry just lost in thought."

"Yeah? Me too."

"What are you thinking about?" I ask curiously. I shouldn't care what he's thinking about I'm not here to ask questions or get closer to him.

"Mostly about kissing you."

My heart freezes inside my chest. Did he just say kissing? Kissing me? I stare at his stupidly handsome face waiting for him to tell me that he was kidding, that it's a joke, but he never does. Instead, he continues talking.

"Would that be okay? If I kiss you, I mean? I know our parents hate each other, and we shouldn't care about each other either, but it's only a kiss." His question hangs in the air for a moment, and I swallow down my nervous anxiety, knowing I'm going to say yes. I don't think I want to kiss him, definitely not, but this is my chance to get close enough to plant the bag.

"Okay.... A kiss... A kiss would be okay, I mean," I whisper right before he brushes a strand of hair from my face. His thumb brushing against my cheek leaving my skin tingling beneath his touch. He leans in, eyes open wide, as if he doesn't want to miss the chance to see my face when our lips touch.

Then our lips touch, pressing together and my eyes close on their own. Tingles of warmth ripple through me. Everything around us fades out as if we are the only two people in the world. All I feel are his soft, full lips against mine. The kiss is gentle, heart-warming, and I lean into him while our lips melt into each other.

I give myself this one second to forget everything, the

reason I am here and the reason I should hate him. Butterflies
flutter around inside my stomach igniting a deep tremble in
my core. A warmth seeps into my bones, melting me like an ice
cream cone sitting in the afternoon sun. I want to get lost in
that feeling, feel nothing else beside it, but my father's voice
rings in my ears right then. I need to remember what his fam-
ily has done, the pain they've caused.

With a heavy heart and an unsteady hand, I grab the
small plastic bag from my pocket and slip it into his before I
pull away breaking the kiss.

My first kiss.

The rattling of keys outside the door drags me
back to reality. The lock clicks and the door opens a moment later. The light flicks on, blinding me in the process.

"What the hell, Harlow?"

I let my eyes adjust for a moment before getting
out of bed and walking over to my friend. "I'm sorry,
Shelby," I say as I throw my arms around her and bury
my face in her thick blonde hair. "I'm really sorry I yelled
at you. You didn't know. I shouldn't have taken it out on
you."

"Didn't know what?" she asks, while wrapping her
own arms around me. "Tell me what's going on, please."

"Okay." Letting go of her, I grab her hand and lead
her to my bed. We sit down together and I wrap the blanket around myself before starting to explain the whole
thing. I swore to my parents I would never tell anyone,
but they don't control me anymore. So, I tell Shelby
about the past, about what happened, and about what
I've done.

I tell her about my greatest shame while hoping
that she can still look at me the same way after. Hoping
that I'm not losing my best friend like I've lost every-

thing else in my life.

CHAPTER THREE

When I open my eyes on the first day of school, I feel better than I thought I would. It's been two days since my encounter with the Bishops and since I spilled the beans about everything to Shelby. She was shocked about the whole thing, but besides that took it pretty well. She didn't hate me like I thought she would and I'm more thankful than ever to have her as my friend. She promised to never say a word about any of it.

Shelby is already gone by the time I'm dressed and ready to go. She has an early class, while mine doesn't start until ten. I briefly thought about switching schools but decided that I'm not going to run from my problems again, Shelby is here and there is no way her father will let her switch schools again and I don't want to go anywhere else by myself. I'm alone as it is, no need to isolate myself further.

I think the best way to deal with the Bishops is to ignore them as best as I can. I won't play into their games or let them bring me down. I came here to be a normal college student and that's what I'm going to be.

Stuffing all my books and notepads into my backpack, I swing it over my shoulder and head out the door, locking it as I go. I turn around and walk down the hallway with a campus map and my class schedule in hand.

With my eyes trained on the paper, I don't even see the person stepping out in front of me until it's too late and my body is crashing into another. Clutching onto the paper in my hands I look up startled.

I'm about to mumble some apology when I realize it's Banks who is towering in front of me, and judging by the expression on his face, him being here isn't just a coincidence.

"Good morning, Princess," he grins, his blue eyes twinkling with one-sided amusement.

"What do you want, Banks?" I try to push past him, but he blocks my exit and steps in my way, with him being built like a brick wall there isn't much I can do to get by him.

"I was just thinking about how nice it would be for me to pick you up so we can walk to our class together."

"*Our* class?" I repeat his words with disbelief.

"Yup, we made sure at least one of us is always in one of your classes, so we can keep an eye on you," he explains. "We wouldn't want you to have a good time or anything." He leans forward brushing a loose strand of hair from my face. His sweet, intoxicating scent of cinnamon wraps around me making it hard for me to breathe. This close I almost forget he's the enemy. *Almost.* "Remember, we're here to make your life as difficult as possible."

"I got that part, thanks." I swat away his hand and twist around walking in the other direction. I'm not doing this. I can't handle it right now.

The sound of his heavy footsteps following me

down the stairs reverberates around the stairwell, but even without the sound, I would know he is there. I can feel his presence. I can feel his body close to mine, just as I can feel each of the Bishop Brothers when they are in the same room as me.

I can't explain it, but it has always been this way. I used to think it was because they were bad and I have a sixth sense about bad people, but I figured out a while ago that the goosebumps covering my skin are not there because they give me the creeps, no it's something much more worrisome than that.

Banks catches up with me and falls into step beside me. My breath hitches at his closeness. Damnit, why does my body have to react this way when one of them is close? Why can't my body get the memo about our mutual hate?

"You are much less annoyed by me being here than I thought you would be. Maybe you even like having me close by," he says, and I can feel my cheeks heating, giving my embarrassment away. "Are you excited to see me? Is that why you didn't pull away when I was standing behind you the other night?"

"Stop," I blurt out and up my pace. Unfortunately, he is much taller than me, his legs longer and even though I'm speed walking now, he is only casually walking next to me, he has no trouble at all keeping up.

Lord, please shove me off the side of a cliff right now.

All I get is two more steps before Banks grabs my arm and pulls me towards him. He twirls us around and pushes my body up against the closest wall. With my back flush against the cold brick, he leans in, so close that his body molds against mine. He dips his head so his mouth is right next to the shell of my ear and I have this strange need, want even, to turn and feel his lips against mine.

Would he kiss me back? This attraction is wrong, but it feels so right.

"Did you like how close I was? How close I am right now?" His breath is hot on my skin and as he talks a shiver runs through my body, from the top of my head all the way down to my toes. This is wrong, so wrong. He is crowding my space, my mind. Making me think and feel things I shouldn't.

Yes. "No," I croak. My lie must not be very convincing, because Banks lets out a soft chuckle at my words. And just like that the moment ends and Banks pulls away, leaving me cold.

"You're still a liar, but that's okay. We'll break you of that nasty little habit."

"Can you just go away?" I try and push down the anger, the shame coursing through me.

"No," he growls. "We won't go away. Not until we are finished with you." He takes a step back, putting a few inches of space between us. "Now, let's go. You might not care about your grades, or classes, but I do, and I don't want to be late on the first day, so get moving or I'll toss you over my shoulder and carry you."

He wouldn't. Would he? My thoughts must be visible on my face.

"Don't tempt me, Harlow. I can, and I will," he whispers so only I can hear him as a group of people walk by. The tone of his voice holds a warning that I shouldn't want to cross but that I feel tempted to.

"Whatever," I sigh, rolling my eyes. If they won't leave me alone, and they feel the need to accompany me to every class, then I'm going to have to come up with a way to make them go away. I'm going to have to come up with a plan.

I'll beat the Bishop Brothers at their own game.

Banks wasn't kidding when he said they made sure that there would be at least one of them in each of my classes. At first, I didn't think they would be that ballsy, but I underestimated them. Their need for revenge is very real. It also makes it very hard for me to focus.

My first class with Banks wasn't so bad, but the one after that with Oliver was horrible. Girls were talking to him the entire time and he was talking back while trying to include me in the conversation, but not in a good way. Of course, when I tried to get them to shut up the professor yelled at me for disrupting the class. By the time lunch comes around I'm annoyed, hungry, and ready to stab all three of them right in the eyes.

"What are we having for lunch, Princess?" Oliver questions as we leave the economics class.

"*We?*" I ask, coming to a stop in the middle of the sidewalk, taking Oliver by surprise. "We aren't having anything for lunch."

Oliver rolls his chocolate brown eyes, "You can fight this all you want but I'm not going anywhere, and neither are my brothers."

He runs a hand through the thick mop of brown hair on his head. I lick my lips, wondering if it's as soft as it looks. Why am I so attracted to these guys? So what I gave Sullivan my first kiss, who cares, that doesn't mean I should want Banks or Oliver.

"God, I'm fucking hungry." Another voice pierces my thoughts, and I whirl around to find Sullivan walking towards us, his lips like a beacon calling out to me.

Jesus. I need to stop thinking about kissing these assholes.

"Well, you're going to be hungry a little longer because princess here says we aren't eating lunch together."

Rolling my eyes, I say, "Neither of you are eating lunch with me. It's bad enough that I can't even attend class by myself. Girls keep looking at me, staring actually, and I can see them sharpening their claws. Being around you guys adds unwanted attention. All I want to do is go to class and go back to my dorm. Is that too much to ask?"

Sullivan crosses the distance between us in a second, the closeness of his body is almost too much for me, his sweet scent wafting into my nostrils. Having all three brothers around me is like sensory overload and I'm seconds away from tapping out.

"That's the point. What do you think it felt like to have all eyes on me? To have people spreading lies about my parents? To be under scrutiny by an entire town?" His words are clipped, and his tone is dark.

Immediately I'm reminded of the seriousness of this situation. I might be daydreaming about kissing them while being annoyed by their presence, but I can't forget why this is happening, how serious the whole thing is. How much they hate me, and how that's the driving force behind everything they do, to see me suffer. I cannot get distracted by my irrational hormonal reaction to them.

My stomach starts to growl then, reminding me

how hungry I am. I could go back to my room and lock myself inside until my next class, maybe they would go away by then. *Doubtful.* But, I have nothing to eat in the dorm.

"Fine," I say defeated. "Let's go get lunch then."

Oliver and Sullivan both smirk triumphantly before escorting me like two wingmen to the campus cafeteria. They make a show of it, opening doors for me like pure gentlemen. I can feel every single pair of eyes on me as we walk. Even the middle-aged lady handing out food is giving me the stink-eye. I want to tell her how much I dislike them following me around but don't. Something tells me she wouldn't care anyway.

When we finally sit down, people at the table next to us start whispering, leaning into each other. I don't know what they're saying but it isn't hard to guess. One of the guys at the table stares at me creepily, and I swear I see him licking his lips as his gaze roams over my chest.

What the fuck?

The girl next to him—who I assume is his girlfriend —gets up to leave, and drags him by his arm out of the cafeteria. If looks could kill, her glare would have struck me dead ten times over.

"Someone might have spread a rumor that you are into some kinky stuff and looking for some more playmates because three guys aren't enough for you," Sullivan snickers before taking a bite of his sandwich. My cheeks heat instantly, and I use my golden hair as a curtain to hide my face from the group of people still sitting at the table nearby.

"You have got to be kidding me," I whisper under my breath. The hunger I felt a minute ago vanishes and is replaced with sickening nausea. I've never even had sex before, and now I'm supposedly into some kinky multiple partner shit?

Shoving away the tray of food I get up to leave.

"Awe, come on, Harlow, it's just a rumor," Oliver teases when I push past him. Grasping on to the strap of my backpack like it could somehow save me, I rush out of the cafeteria, hoping that they'll give me a little space. I need some time to myself, a few seconds to breathe and gather my thoughts.

Darting around the building I lean against the brick wall and press my hands to my hot face. Coming here was supposed to help me forget about my past, about North Woods, about all the things I did for my father, but I should have known better than to be so hopeful. I couldn't just run away from what I've done, away from my problems. It didn't mean I didn't want to try though.

After a few minutes of breathing exercises, I finally succeed in calming down enough to think properly. Running a hand over my face and through my hair, I hope that I look like a normal person and not someone who is on the verge of a mental breakdown.

Straightening up I walk back around the building. Looking at my phone in shock, I realize I've been hiding out behind the building way longer than I thought.

Shit. I'm going to be late for my next class. Still looking down at my phone since there is a text from Shelby that I need to return, I start walking in the direction of the science building when I hear someone calling my name.

I'm grateful that it's not one of the brothers. This voice is feminine.

"Hey, Harlow," the voice is familiar and when I

look up from my phone I spot the girl from the other night. *Caroline?* I think that's her name, the tinker bell lookalike.

"Hi, Caroline," I greet, "Sorry, but I'm running late. I have to get to the science building."

"Environmental science 101?"

My brows furrow with confusion, "Ah, yeah. How did you know?"

"I'm heading to the same class," she giggles, her brown head bopping. "I guess we'll be late together then."

For the first time today I smile, because the brothers' are nowhere in sight, and I'm venturing out, making friends. The walk to class is a short one, but Caroline packs our walk full of questions. Like where I'm from, if I'm really dating all three of the Bishop Brothers? Apparently rumors spread faster than I thought in college.

We make it to class five minutes after it starts. The professor gives me a sour look but doesn't say anything. My gaze sweeps around the class to find a seat, more eyes, and whispers.

Great. Only two chairs are free and of course Banks is sitting next to one of those free ones. He gives me a strangely warm smile, waving me over. Jesus, why can't they just go away. I shake my head at him, but then watch Caroline take the other free chair, leaving me with no other option.

"Please take a seat, Miss," The professor scolds, annoyance lacing his words.

With my head bowed in defeat, I slump down next to Banks and open my text book.

"Can I join your harem, Harlow?" Banks asks, and I

know he's just being a dick, rubbing the rumor in my face. Using my elbow I hit him in the side, and smile when he lets out a low grunt, letting me know that he didn't see that one coming. Caroline gives me a bewildered expression, and I wonder if she believes me or the rumors being spread?

Banks' jaw tightens, and his eyes narrow as he leans down to whisper in my ear.

"Elbow me again and I'll make a mockery out of you in front of everyone." His warning makes me shiver and I can't help but turn slightly, my gaze colliding with his. The need to ask him what he would do is almost too much. My mind imagining all kinds of things, all of which are wrong in every way.

There's a hurricane of emotions swirling in those blue depths and I want to crack him open, spill all his secrets. Sullivan might have had my first kiss, but something tells me Banks will have my second.

A flurry of whispers fill the room and I realize people are looking at us, smiling, laughing and just like that I've made a mistake. I've fed right into the rumors being spread. The grin that spreads across Banks' smug face tells me that was his point all along and suddenly I'm back to hating him and his brothers all over again.

CHAPTER FOUR

The first week of classes passes without another incident. Other than dirty looks and whispering everywhere I go nothing else has happened and, thank god for that. I have enough to deal with as it is.

I hate to admit it, but classes are harder than I thought. I had always had good grades in high school without even trying too much and I just now realize that it might have had something to do with my dad being a huge donor to school funding.

"How are you holding up?" Shelby asks, while I'm getting ready for a shower. I shrug. Really not sure what the hell I should tell her. Do I tell her about the brothers following me around? About the rumors? I'm sure she has already heard them.

"Everything is okay, I guess, I just imagined college would be different," I admit. "I thought it would be the two of us having fun, spending our days doing whatever we wanted," Shelby is studying art, while I'm majoring in social psychology. I knew we wouldn't have a lot of classes together, but I didn't expect to see her so little.

"I know the guys are getting on your nerves."

"That's the understatement of the year," I scoff.

"They just won't let up. I don't know where they get the energy to be so annoying."

"Oh man, that sounds bad." She shakes her head. "I can't believe I used to have a crush on Sullivan."

"You did?" I can't believe I didn't know that.

"Yeah, sixth grade, Miss Holli's class."

I shrug. "Well, don't feel bad, everybody had a crush on him in middle school."

"Yeah, I guess. Hey, listen, I'm sorry we're not spending much time together, and I'm even more sorry for what I'm about to tell you."

"Oh god, what is it? Is something wrong? Is your dad making you move back?" I don't think I can take anything else right now. We might not see each other very much but knowing she is here, with me, it makes me feel better, not so alone.

"No, no, it's not that. It's just..." She seems to skirt around it, and the knot of anxiety in my gut starts to build. "It's just... I got a paid internship at the local art gallery." She finally mutters, head hanging low, as if she's ashamed.

"Oh my god, Shelby! That's great! I'm so proud of you," I screech, lunging towards her and throwing my arms around her neck. "Wait. Why do you sound so sad about it?" She should be excited, jumping up and down, but instead she looks like one of those dogs in the animal shelter.

"Because it means that I'll be gone even more. We will hardly see each other, and I know you need me right now. I'm being a bad friend. I should just decline the offer. I'm only a freshman and I don't really need the money either."

I start to shake my head, blonde strands of hair

cling to my face.

"Oh, hell no. You will absolutely not! You will go and rock their world and show them how amazing you are."

No way will I allow her to give something like this up, she deserves to have freedom too. I'll survive, one way or another. She's not going to sacrifice her happiness to be a human shield for me.

"Are you sure? I came here for you, and I don't want to be that friend that skips out."

"Yes, I'm sure. If you don't go, I will make you." I give her my best evil look which only makes me smile. She examines my face like she doesn't believe me, and I narrow my gaze, seriousness overtaking my features.

"Okay! I'll go," she murmurs into my hair as she leans forward. I hold onto her a little longer before pulling away, missing the hug as soon as it ends. "They're asking me to come in today so they can show me around, after classes I'll head over there, and be back later tonight. Maybe we can get a later dinner together or something?"

"Yes, that would be great. And just so you know, I'm so proud of you. You deserve this. Now go and have fun. I have to take a shower anyway. In case you haven't noticed, I stink," I exclaim, fake smelling my armpit as I grab my shower bag.

Shelby pulls back completely, pinching her nose. "That's what that smell is."

"Hey, now!" I complain, giggling.

"Get out of here and get rid of that smell." She teases. Slipping from the room feeling lighthearted and happy I head down the hall to the showers. That's one of the many crappy things about living in dorms, the bathrooms are shared, and so are the showers.

I walk into the bathroom and find two other girls inside glancing at me like they are unhappy to see me. I'm not even in the shower yet and I can hear two girls whispering in the corner. I don't know if they just don't care or if they are making it obvious on purpose but it's annoying as hell. All the rumors, and whispers are soul-sucking. I thought it would die down after a couple of days, but it seems the more I ignore it the louder the whispers get. The fact that one of the brothers is with me at all times just adds to the rumor mill.

Trying my best to ignore them I strip out of my clothes and set them down on the bench in front of the showers.

The sound of a door opening and closing meets my ears right before I slip out of my underwear and get into the shower stall, pulling the curtain closed behind me. Hopefully that was them leaving, as the last thing I want to do is deal with catty bitches after a shower. Fiddling with the water I wait till it turns hot and let the steamy water soothe my stiff neck muscles. As I wash my hair the silence inside the large room becomes too much and I start humming to myself.

Lost in the shower and the song inside my head, I don't hear someone come into the room.

"What song is that, Princess?" A male voice echoes around me. I'm so startled I drop my soap and almost slip and land on my ass in the process. Thankfully I'm able to grab onto the shower curtain and steady myself before I do. With my heart racing out of my chest, and my eyes wide I stand there, shocked, and confused.

Fisting the flimsy plastic in my hand, I pull the curtain to the side just enough to stick my head out and find Banks standing right in front of my shower stall with a smug grin, and a mischievous glint in his eyes. Even though I'm annoyed, I can't help the warm flush that works its way through me at the sight of him. He's wearing a tight fitted T-shirt, and a pair of ripped jeans that hug his toned legs. He looks like he belongs on a magazine cover.

"What the hell are you doing?" I bark.

"Just checking up on you. Making sure you're cleaning all the important spots." His eyes roam over my curtain covered body and even though I know he can't see through the blue plastic, I feel like he can. In the presence of the Bishop Brothers it's like being under a microscope and right now I feel naked and exposed and the worst part is that I'm not embarrassed or appalled by it, not at all.

In fact, I'm curious, excited, and a little turned on.

Bad, Harlow. Bad. I internally scold myself.

"You want me to join?" he asks, a thick brown brow raised. His question making me gulp. *Yes. Yes, I do.* Wait... no... no I don't. When I don't answer him right away, he takes a step towards me.

"N-No... Please leave, you're not supposed to be in here. This is a girls' only bathroom." I state the obvious, trying very hard not to imagine Banks stripping out of his clothes and stepping into the shower with me. Briefly I wonder which of the brothers looks better without their shirts on, who has the bigger...

"Whatever." He shrugs, the blazing fire in his eyes turning to ice in an instant. "Your loss."

"Get out, Banks, or I'm going to report you to the RA."

"Oooo, I'm so scared," he taunts.

We both know it wouldn't matter if I reported him. It's already obvious the Bishops are royalty at Bayshore. I wonder what kind of donation their parents gave the school, god knows new students, freshman at that, wouldn't hold sway like they do.

Pulling the curtain shut all the way, making sure that there isn't even an inch of space at the sides for him to peek in I finish washing my body, keeping my eyes on the shower curtain at all times. Eventually, I hear his heavy footfalls walking away from me, my heart beats a little more, but only when I hear the door open and shut does it steady to a normal rhythm.

I finish showering, shaving my legs, and washing my hair, before stepping out of the shower. I freeze when I look down on the bench where I deposited all of my stuff. Gone. My clothes are gone. My towel is *gone*. That asshole took everything.

I'm standing completely naked and alone in the center of the room, staring at the bench waiting for my stuff to reappear. Moments pass, water droplets still dripping down my body. When I am completely certain that this is reality and I'm not just stuck in a bad dream, I start going through the lockers, hoping, and praying that there is something to cover myself with. At least so I can get to my room.

When I get to the twentieth locker I finally find a towel. It's small, old, and smells horrendous, but it's better than nothing. I don't dry my hair. I just wrap the nasty towel around my body and head back to my room. The scratchy thing is so small it barely covers all my lady parts.

By some kind of freaking miracle no one is in the

hallway and I make it to my room without incident. I get to my door and halt for a split second. I don't have my key either, it was in my bag that Banks took, and I don't remember if I locked the door or not. I turn the knob, saying a silent prayer and thanking the universe when the door opens.

Quickly I rush inside, closing my eyes I lean against the door and sigh loudly.

Thank goodness.

"Lose something?" A deep gravelly voice calls. *oh, no, he didn't! He couldn't, right?*

Wide-eyed I spin around clutching the barely there towel to my chest. I'm pretty sure my ass cheeks are showing but it's better than my tits or vagina. I can't believe Banks has the nerve to be here after what he just did. Asshole.

"You." My bottom lip curls with anger when I see him lounging on my bed, a shit eating grin spread across his face.

"Me?" He huffs out a laugh, "What about me? I've been sitting here the whole time waiting for you. It seems you forgot to take your things with you? How is that my fault?" The smile, the fact that he's sitting there looking handsome, and put together while I'm barely hanging on by a thread enrages me.

"Listen, I can deal with you following me around like lost puppies and even the rumors that I know you and your brothers are spreading about me, but this shit, this little stunt goes too far! You need to stay out of my room and out of the showers." I'm so angry, my hands are shaking. *How dare he?* I should have known they would step up their game. That they would do more than just spread rumors and follow me around. This is the last place I have left, my oasis. The only place I can go to get away from them. I can handle a lot of things but this... this invasion of privacy. It's the last straw.

"You crossed the line, Banks!" I yell, feeling my skin heat at the outburst.

"*I...I crossed the line?*" Banks is suddenly on his feet, and across the room before I can even blink, stopping only inches away from me. The air between us grows thick, making it hard to breath. With his thick finger pointed right at my chest he continues, "You would know all about crossing the line, wouldn't you? About making up lies, and ruining someone's future, their life?" I hadn't ruined Sullivan's life, had I?

"Looks like you're all living a great life, so it couldn't have been that bad..."

"Wasn't that bad, huh?" he mutters to himself in disbelief, "Do you have any idea what you've done to our family? How devastated Sullivan was that he was kicked from the team. People..." He doesn't finish what he says and I'm not sure I want him to. I don't need to hear anything else. I know what I did was wrong, hell, I knew it was wrong before I did it.

When he looks up at me his features are menacing, and I know I should probably be scared right now, but I'm not. Him being this close to me and me being so exposed has my body vibrating with foreign excitement. His heady scent invades my nostrils and all I can think of is him. I forget his anger, forget my guilt, and shame. Everything falls away, leaving just us.

Releasing my hold on the towel I let my arms fall to the sides of my body. Cool air washes over my bare skin, and my nipples harden to tight peaks.

I don't know who is more shocked by what I just

did, me or him? I watch his eyes soften and darken at the same time. His pupils dilate as his gaze drops between us, his gaze wanders over my naked form. I watch his chest rise and fall at a faster pace than normal, matching my own erratic breathing.

Shit, I shouldn't have done that.

When his gaze shoots back up and our eyes meet there is a spark there, and that spark ignites an entire fire inside me. Without thinking I take a step forward at the same time as he does. Our lips meet in a furious, almost punishing kiss. There is an urgency to this kiss, and it's completely unlike the one I experienced with Sullivan. Its rage and anger, and I feel like if I don't continue kissing him right now I might combust.

Snaking my arms around his neck I pull him closer. My nipples brush against the soft fabric of his shirt, and I damn near moan at the sensation. His hands easily find my hips and he pulls me closer, so close there isn't a millimeter of space left between us. I can feel my core pulsing, my body melting into his. I know he wants me, the hardened bulge in his jeans telling me so. We continue to kiss, his lips pressing against mine, his hands holding onto me with a possessiveness that excites and terrifies me.

He nips at my bottom lip and I moan feeling the bite deep in my core. I want him, need him. Blood rushes in my ears, and then it ends. Like a cold bucket of water has been tipped over me. Banks pulls away pushing me backwards. I sway unsteadily on my legs. His lips are wet and swollen and all I want to do is run my fingers over them.

"No! You're not going to pull that shit on me," he growls, shaking his head in annoyance. "This might have worked on Sullivan, but you can't use the same trick twice and expect no one to notice."

"He told you?" I respond hoarsely, lust still clogging my throat. My lips swollen and my skin burning where he touched me.

Grinning, he says, "Of course he told us, we're his brothers. Now keep your lips, and your body to yourself, because next time I won't stop. Next time, I'll take and take until there isn't anything left."

Without another look, he pushes me out of the way and exits the room. Bringing a hand to my lips I can still feel his kiss there, the heat of his body burning into mine and I know I'll be thinking about him for a long while to come.

CHAPTER FIVE

Four days pass without Banks showing himself. My little towel stunt must have had some type of impact on him because he no longer follows me around. That doesn't mean I'm allowed to roam around on my own though. Sullivan and Oliver still escort me every place I go. By now, I'm getting used to it. I'm also getting used to the way people gawk at me and the snotty remarks that follow. Turns out college is just like high school, only with more people and less consequences.

"Where are you going?" Oliver asks, falling into step beside me. He's the oldest of the Bishops, and I like to tell myself the smartest. When it comes to cracking them, Oliver will be the hardest nut. "This is not the way to your dorm."

"Great observation skills, Sherlock. I'm going to the library," I snap, hoping it will deter him enough that he will leave me alone. I can't concentrate when one of them is close by and I really need to write this paper. It wouldn't be a problem to do it at my dorm, but the professor is adamant about only using library sources so it's either the library or a failing grade.

"I'll help you study," he snickers, and I already

know he is going to do the opposite.

"Look, if you don't let me do this…" I stop, because I don't want to sound weak, or give them any more ammunition, but I also don't really have anything to threaten him with nor do I want to. "I will fail this class if I don't go to the library and then I'll have to leave the school. How will you make my life a living nightmare if I'm not going to school here anymore? Huh?" I mock, the idea of dropping out wouldn't be so bad if I didn't have to face my father.

"We'll just follow you wherever you go," he says nonchalantly, as if he's already thought the scenario through.

"Even back to my parents?"

Oliver's gaze turns dark and he cuts me off midstep, my body colliding with his, causing me to bounce back off of him. I can feel myself falling backwards when his arm circles my waist and he pulls me into his chest. "Oh, we won't let you get away that easily. We're done here when we say we're done and not a moment sooner. Do you understand?"

This close I can see just how beautiful he truly is, high cheekbones, a strong, sharp jaw, and full lips that draw you in. His hair is a disheveled glossy mass of russet brown that I want to run my fingers through.

Enemy. Bully. Rival. I repeat inside my head, to starve off the indecent thoughts I'm having right now.

"Harlow," Oliver calls out, and I shake myself from the daze I'm in. The dimpled smile on his face tells me I've been caught red-handed.

"You know, I thought Banks was joking when he said you threw yourself at him, but I see it now. That's your thing, isn't it? You use your body to get what you want? How many guys have you slept with to get your way?"

I can't help but laugh at his question as I push him away. I'm a little insulted and for a split second I think about telling him that I'm still a virgin, but that fact seems too personal to share, especially with him.

"Oh no! You got me." I raise my hands into the air like an idiot. "Harlow, the harlot. I just go around kissing guys and whisking them off into my bed to get them to do what I want. Haven't you heard," I lean into his stoic face, "my vagina is made of gold."

His facial expression combined with the words I'm spewing send me into a fit of laughter that makes my belly hurt. Bending over I hold a hand to my stomach and snort loudly.

"Fucking Christ," he mumbles under his breath, grabbing me by the arm and practically dragging me up the steps to the library.

"I'm guessing you didn't think that was funny?"

We pass a group of people and even with the quick motion I can still feel their eyes on me. Once up the steps I shake off his hold and put some space between us.

"You aren't taking this serious at all, are you?" he asks, his voice threaded with frustration. Little does he know his frustration only makes me feel better. Shrugging, I tuck a couple loose strands of hair behind my ear. My chest is still burning from the laughter and the run up the steps. "This is all a game to you. That's all it's ever been."

"I guess it doesn't really matter what my answer is. You guys will do your worst no matter what I say." I don't wait around to hear his response. Instead I turn and walk inside the library. *My sanctuary.*

Oliver follows behind me like there is an invisible string tethered between us. It doesn't take me long to find a seat, and I pull out the chair making sure I don't scrape it against the wooden floor.

"I'm giving you one hour, that's it. Then I'm putting you over my shoulder and carrying you back to the dorm. I'm not babysitting your ass all night." He growls, throwing himself into one of the wooden chairs. He almost looks too small for it.

"Aww, why not? Got another girl to traumatize?" I whisper getting my notes, pencils, and book out.

"Nope, only you," he says, and somehow his words make their way into my brain and make me feel a way I'm sure he didn't intend. *Only you.*

I start working on the stupid paper, trying to concentrate on my books and not on Oliver sitting next to me. A few times I have to get up and find different books for references, and every time I do, Oliver's there watching me like a hawk, like I'm some criminal that's about to make a run for it or something.

After almost an hour I'm not even close to being done.

Sighing, I set my pencil down. "You know you don't *have* to babysit me, right? I'm not anywhere near being done here and it's painfully obvious you don't want to be here. I don't understand why you have to watch me every second of the day. I'm not a child."

At my words he looks up from his phone, which he's been playing with for the better part of the last hour.

"No, I have a better idea. You gather your stuff up and we'll head back to your dorm. I gave you an hour of my time, if you want more you'll have to earn it." His expression is dead serious, nothing but honesty reflecting in his eyes and that kind of frightens me.

"*Earn it?* What's that supposed to mean? If you think I'm going to sleep with you, then you're mentally ill."

"Pfft, you'd be lucky to ever get graced with such an amazing experience."

I stare at him, my expression blank, "I'm not earning anything. I'm a grown person and if I want to stay here then I will. I'm a human, not an object." I barely get the words out before he is on his feet and reaching across the table. He gathers my papers and pencils stuffing them into my backpack haphazardly.

"Stop," I demand. "I'm not done!" I'm vaguely aware of someone saying *shhhh* but I'm more concerned with Oliver than them right at this moment.

"I don't care. We're leaving." He grits out, and I worry I may have pushed him too far this time. Out of the corner of my eye I spot the librarian getting up from her desk. *Oh shit!* She starts walking toward us, casting a glare our way that says *shut up or get out.*

"I'm serious, I'm not going. I need to finish this paper," I whisper yell as I reach for my backpack.

Oliver's expression turns deadly. "And I'm serious, as well. Walk out or I'll walk you out." I want to slap him so badly, but right then the librarian walks up.

"You two need to leave, right now!" The librarian who looks older than the building scolds, her finger pointing back and forth between us.

"He needs to leave." I hook my thumb in Oliver's direction. "I'm staying. I'm sure you could see I've been working for the last hour. He hasn't."

Before anyone can respond, Oliver zips up my bag, swings it over his shoulder and then squats down, while grabbing onto my hips he tosses me over his shoulder like I'm nothing more than a sack of potatoes. I start to squeal like a pig as soon as I'm in the air.

"Put me down, right now!" I order.

"Out!" The librarian demands. "And don't come back."

"What? I didn't do anything," I yell through the otherwise silent library as Oliver carries me out like a caveman. I'm flustered, irritated, and confused. Balling my hands into fists I start pounding on his back, but it doesn't seem to even phase him. He just continues walking like he's taking a long peaceful stroll through the park.

"Put me down! So help me god, Oliver," I growl.

"Quiet or I'll spank you."

"Excuse me?" I squeak, unsure of how I feel about that.

"You heard me."

"You wouldn't dare. Now put me…" My words are cut off by Oliver's hand as it comes down hard on my ass cheek.

Holy shit, he spanked me. I beat on his back harder, hoping that I'll leave him with bruises, or at least something to remember me by.

"I hate you!" I growl.

"Sure you do," he chuckles into the night air.

We're halfway across campus when I finally give up, exhausted from pounding on his back and getting nowhere, I just slump down on his shoulder. Then I realize that people must have seen the scene in the library followed by Oliver carrying me across campus on his shoulder. This literally couldn't get any worse.

He walks me into my dorm, stopping in my hallway to set me down. I'm still unsteady on my feet, try-ing to regain my bearings after hanging upside down on the way over here, when I'm suddenly pushed against the wall.

"Do you really hate me, Harlow?" Oliver asks, his fingers moving under my chin to tip it upwards, forcing me to look up and into his eyes. With all the hard plains of his body pressing up against mine it's hard to think or breathe.

My tongue feels like a weight is attached to it. I can't form words, there's something wrong with me, something very wrong.

Oliver grins and then leans down pressing his lips against mine. Our lips crash together like a tidal wave against a cliff. My hands come up landing on his chest and for a brief second I consider pushing him away. I should, my heart is already a mess, my mind in complete dis-array. Slowly they're breaking me down, and I'm letting them.

Against my better judgement I cave to my body's need, and instead of pushing him away my fingers clench onto the fabric of his shirt to pull him closer. Again, the kiss is different in comparison to his brothers. Oliver kisses with passion, with a longing that you feel deep down in your soul.

All the anger I felt towards him melts away and is left somewhere in a puddle on the floor. His hands find my hips, pulling me into him. His hardened cock presses against my thigh making my mouth water. My whole body is on fire. His tongue slides across my bottom lip, begging for entry and without hesitation I part my lips, a tiny moan escaping in the process.

The second our tongues touch I'm done for. He

tastes like sweet mint and forbidden fruit and I'm reminded of how wrong all of this is, but I can't help wanting him. It's like I'm possessed or something. Like a goddamn dog in heat, I want all three of the brothers.

The blood in my ears roars and I bite at Oliver's lip, the growl that emits from his throat shoots straight to my core, and I clutch onto him harder. This is bad, but it's so much better than all the fighting and hating. I like this, this place where we only exist in the moment, without anyone or anything living in the same world.

Of course, as soon as I start to think that, the moment between us ends.

Oliver pulls away, leaving me breathless, with my swollen lips burning for him.

"Fuck, my brothers were right, you do taste sinful, but oddly sweet too." His eyes reflect hunger and when he swipes at his bottom lip with his thumb I nearly come undone.

He takes a step back to leave, and somehow I find my voice, "Wait, don't leave."

"Stay in your dorm. If I find out you left, I'm spanking that sexy ass until its red." My gaze widens partially because he's so straight forward about the punishment and partially because I kinda want to break the rules just to see if he'll do it.

"But..."

He shakes his head, and lifts a brow in warning, "Be a good girl now." The words come out in a whisper and before I can muster up a response he's gone, walking down the hall. I stare at his back until he's out of sight and then sigh against the door.

What the hell just happened?

"Oh my god, you're totally sleeping with all three

of them. Wow, you really are a slut. I better not catch you trying to seduce my boyfriend with one of your kinky fuck fests." Some girl I failed to notice standing in the hall snarls. Horror, shock, and disgust reflect in her features.

Jesus, how long has she been standing there? Scrubbing a hand down my face I ignore her, and only then do I realize that the boys have slowly been making the rumors worse, showing up here, kissing me, leaving my dorm at random times. I thought it was bad having them follow me around but now they're kissing me, touching me, and my body is short circuiting.

"Holy hell," I mumble to myself.

My breathing is still uneven, and my lips feel like they are on fire. Maybe I should heed Oliver's warning, but I really need to get that paper done, I need to get to the library and apologize to the librarian, begging her to let me in. I reach for my backpack—My blood pressure spikes—my backpack, that little shit took my bag with him. I don't even think as I run down the hall, and around the corner to the door.

That asshole with his stupidly good kissing skills distracted me. Shoving the door open I step out into the night, cool air kissing my heated cheeks. I look around the well-manicured lawn looking for anyone that might look like Oliver but find no one.

It's eerily quiet. *Motherfuck!* Descending the steps, I start to head in the direction of the library. I have no way of getting out to their mansion, so I hope he hasn't left campus yet. Along the way I silently scold myself. I'm stupid, so stupid. I let my hormones rule me again. I have got to stop thinking with my vagina. I'm supposed to dislike the Bishop Brothers, not want to ride them like Channing Tatum in the *Magic Mike* movie.

Caught up in my own thoughts I round the corner and collide with another body, a body that's much larger, much beefier than my own. The impact causes me to bounce like a bouncy ball of off the person and land harshly on the concrete sidewalk.

"Ugh." I whine, an ache radiating up my spine. My night goes from bad to worse when I find Sullivan staring down at me. His face lit by the soft glow of the street lamp above us.

"Weren't you told to stay in your dorm?" he accuses, like I'm a child sneaking out and he's my parent.

"The gentleman thing to do would be to apologize and then help me up," I spit coldly, my eyes lingering on him a little longer than they should. *Stop staring.* Stop staring, Harlow. He's got his hands tucked into a pair of worn jeans, and he's wearing a dark Henley that shows off his toned chest, and biceps perfectly.

Boo, why can't they stop looking gorgeous, and while they're at it stop following me around too. These shenanigans are getting old.

"I'm not a gentleman, but I thought you already knew that?" The boyish grin he gives me makes my heart start to race. If these three don't stop fucking with me, I'll be going into cardiac arrest. I feel like every time I escape the frying pan one of them finds me and tosses me back into the fire. It's beyond exhausting.

"Ain't that the truth," I mumble under my breath, I still have the throbbing pain in my spine, but I push through and get up off the sidewalk. I wipe my sweaty hands on the front of my skinny jeans.

"I don't need a babysitter, so you can go and do whatever it is you brothers do when you aren't making my life hell."

"You like us making your life hell."

Narrowing my gaze, I say, "Do not. All I want is to be left alone. I came here to forget about my past, and then you show up here, and ruin everything."

Sullivan shrugs his sculpted shoulders, "I'd say I'm sorry but I'm not. You fucked me over that night, Harlow." He takes a step forward, his huge hand reaching out for me, cupping my cheek gently. I should pull away, run back to my dorm, but I can't. I crave their attention as much as I hate it. I need more, so much more.

"I thought you were different, sweet, and innocent. That night, I was sure I saw a glimpse of a girl that cared, and then like a snake slithering through the grass you showed your true self, sinking your teeth into my skin, injecting me with a nasty venom," he snarls, and even angry he looks beautiful, like a tall wave and I'm the coastline standing in his way.

"I...." My tongue darts out over my bottom lip and his gaze hones in on the movement. The muscles in his throat tightening as he swallows.

"You're a temptress, and I'm weak, so fucking weak for you," he whispers, leaning forward, his hot breath fanning against my lips.

Kiss me. I think to myself, but then decide to take charge pushing up onto my tiptoes I brush my lips against his. A groan resonates from somewhere deep inside of him, and his free hand moves to my hip. My shirt rides up with the movement and I gasp at the feel of his hand on my bare skin. Ahh, it feels heavenly.

"You want me, don't you?" There's a huskiness to his voice and I nod my head, unable to form a single word. There's something in the back of my mind that tells me this is a bad idea, but I push the thought away. All I want is to feel wanted, loved, cared for, and in some twisted way the Bishop Brothers make me feel all those things, even if they don't realize it.

With a gentle nudge he pushes me against the side of the building and out of the street lamp light. It's harder to see him this way, but not impossible. I can still hear his heavy breathing and feel the hardness of his body brushing against all my softness. Everything is different between us this time, the very first time he kissed me he was gentle, kind, unsure. But this time there's a darkness that clings to him, and I want that darkness to overtake me, to claim me.

He Slides his hand from my hip up my body, until he's cupping my breast through the silky fabric of my bra. My knees shake as molten lava pools in my belly when he flicks his thumb over the hardened nub.

"Sometimes, at night when I can't sleep, I think about what you look like when you come. And I wonder, do you think about just me, or me and my brothers?"

"Oh god," I sigh, my core tightening around nothing but air. I want his fingers there, his tongue, his... it dawns on me then, do I really want him to be my first?

All the thoughts inside my head become fuzzy when he flicks his finger over my nipple again, and leans forward, peppering my throat with hot kisses. Kisses that turn into something more, and soon he's sucking on the tender flesh below my ear. Eliciting quiet mewls of pleasure out of me. Like a tiny kitten I claw at him, pulling him closer.

Lost in my own little bubble of joy, I don't notice someone approaching until a throat is being cleared right beside us.

Oh my god! Without thought I'm shoving at Sullivan's chest. He takes a step back, chest heaving, eyes flickering with fire as he stares down at me with confusion. Without his body shielding mine two girls come into view. They both wear the same look of disgust and I notice then that there's also a guy with them.

"You done with her brother?"

I blink, and for some reason betrayal cuts deep into the tender tissue of my heart hearing Oliver's voice. He's with two girls. He was in a hurry to get away from me to be with them.

"Yeah, you done with that, Sullivan?" One of them snickers. Tears glisten in my eyes. I couldn't stop them from forming even if I wanted to. There's a sick feeling that coats my insides at being caught out here, letting him feel me up like some cheap whore.

Something that looks an awful lot like shame flickers in Sullivan blue depths but before I can read him completely a mask falls into place, overtaking his true emotions. He takes a step back, the street lamp above emitting a soft glow over his features.

"Of course, I'm done. Thanks for the fun, Harlow." The cruelness in his eyes leaves me cold, and I barely keep it together as he gives me one last once over before walking away with his brother and their groupies. Squeezing my eyes shut I tell myself that I won't cry, that I don't care what those girls think of me or how the brothers are using my attraction towards them to make things worse.

After that, I care about nothing, not the paper I need to finish, not the rumors or the betrayal I'm feeling. The boys don't own me, and I don't own them, but it feels like something has changed and I don't know how to deal with all the feelings I'm having.

They're bullies, and I'm the victim of their torment, so why do I feel like falling to my knees for them? Why does seeing them with someone else feel like my heart is being ripped out of my chest?

CHAPTER SIX

Banks returns to Harlow duty after the embarrassment of the other night. He doesn't mention our kiss, and I hate to admit it but after what happened with Sullivan and Oliver I kind of missed him.

"Why the sad face?" he asks.

I shrug, "Aren't you supposed to be making my life hell? Not asking me why I'm sad? That kind of defeats the entire purpose, doesn't it?"

"Maybe I want to be the one making you sad."

"Don't worry, you and your brothers are the main cause of my misery, so rest assured, you are doing your job. Three golden stars for the assholes that follow me around like they have nothing better to do with their time." It's harder today to hide the disdain I feel for them. Especially since there's a giant hickey on the side of my neck.

I tried everything I could to cover it up, but nothing seems to conceal the purple and red splotch on my pale skin.

"Feisty. Maybe you just need to relax a little, then again from the hickey on your neck maybe you're doing a little too *much* relaxing?" My face deadpans, I'm so close to losing it and punching him, that it's scary.

"Stop following me," I snap and pick up my pace, my shoes smacking against the concrete. The world wouldn't be turning if he couldn't annoyingly keep up with me, and for a second I think about breaking out into a full on sprint. Then again with Banks' long legs and fitness level, I wouldn't be surprised if he ran circles around me.

He blatantly ignores my attitude and continues talking like I haven't said anything at all.

"Oh, I know the perfect thing. How about a party? You could learn to live a little. All you do is go to your classes, and back to your dorm."

Blinking slowly, I have half a mind to say, *I wonder why,* but I don't because I don't want to engage in any more of a verbal sparring match than I have to.

"That's a hard pass. Thanks for asking," I murmur sarcastically. There is no way in Hell I'm going to a party with him or his brothers. That's practically begging for something bad to happen.

"Suit yourself. But don't whine and cry later on claiming you never get to do anything." Seriously, he sounds like a mixture between my dad and a prison warden.

"I wouldn't give you the pleasure of seeing me cry," I sneer, trying not to notice him, or his toned body. My first mistake was kissing them, my second was enjoying it, because now that I've kissed them, and touched them, my body calls for more, a low warmth simmering deep in my belly every time they're near.

It's annoying, but it also makes me curious.

"Have a totally lame night, Harlow," Banks snorts, as we arrive at my dorm and he shoves his hands into the front pockets of his jeans. *Don't look at him.* Don't let his good looks mess with your head. He's a bully, the enemy, an asshole with a nice face, that's it.

Rolling my eyes I grab my keys and unlock the door.

"Go away, and don't come back." I growl. As soon as I enter the room Shelby jumps up from her bed and runs over to me. I slam the door closed in Banks' face and feel a tiny sliver of power ripple through me.

"Surprise!" She squeals.

"Hey, I thought you'd be gone all night?" I greet and give her a quick hug.

"I know, but then the art show got moved to next week and I wanted to come and surprise my best friend because I miss her, and I'm not the only surprise," her smile widens. "I got us invited to a boat party!" Her eyes light up, and she's beaming like it's the most exciting thing she's ever heard. "A boat party, Harlow! I'm not going to take no for an answer, so don't even waste your time saying it, and if you're worried about the Bishop boys, I'll help you ditch them."

I can't stop the sigh that passes my lips. I don't want to go to a party but I really don't want to disappoint Shelby either. The guys will be there, there's no doubt about it, and if I show up they'll most likely follow me around. On the other hand, I can't keep hiding out in my dorm doing nothing every weekend because of them.

If I stay home, they win. Plus, parties are part of college life, right? I should enjoy this time of my life to the fullest.

Shelby crosses her arms over her chest and gives me the look. What look you ask? The one that shows her annoyance and precedes an hour-long lecture about how

I won't always be young, and able to make dumb choices. Her mouth pops open as if she's about to start talking but I cut her off.

"Okay, I'll go," I say and watch her face turn from stern to surprised, and then to excited.

"Holy shit, I was prepared to do some major sweet talking, and a whole lot of persuasion to get you to go, but this thing where you agree so easily is much better. If only you could be this easy all the time."

"If I was that easily convinced then it would be no fun."

"True, and since you didn't take up all my time with talking, we now have more time to pick out dresses," she giggles and runs to the closet. As She starts dragging one dress after the other out of the closet and creating a line up on her bed, I take a seat on the edge of mine.

Crossing my legs, I wait for her to give me my choice for tonight. My phone starts to buzz in my pocket. I dread even looking at it, somehow the guys got my phone number and when they are not busy walking me across campus, they send me text messages or call me. They're the worst.

"I can hear the phone vibrating from over here," Shelby says over her shoulder, "who is it? One of your Romeos?"

"Romeos? Not you too. You know I'm not actually with any of them, right? They are just stalking me to get on my nerves and under my skin."

"Sure, they are."

My brows furrow together in a frown. "What's that supposed to mean?"

She whirls around, a mini skirt in her hands. "Why

do you let them stalk you? Did you even try to talk to campus security or the dean's office, or even the police? I mean, they are legit stalking you, but you don't do anything about it, so maybe you don't *want* to be with them, but it's not like you're stopping them either."

Because I deserve it. I think to myself, but the words won't actually leave my mouth, I'm too ashamed to admit how I feel. Instead, I tell her the other reason I haven't said anything yet. "You know how it is, Shelby. They have tons of money, do you really think they haven't thought about this? Haven't made a sizable donation to the school to make sure that they can do no wrong? Plus, the second I say something they'll retaliate by doing something even worse."

"What could be worse than what they've already done? It's not like they would physically harm you. They're a bunch of ankle biting dogs."

"Says the one not being followed by them everywhere she goes."

"Do you want me to say something to them?"

Scrubbing a hand down the front of my face, I mutter, "God, no. Let them do their thing. They only win if I let them. Once they see that I won't react, they'll just give up and move on. I mean, how fun can it be following a girl around all day? Surely they'll get bored of this soon enough?"

She laughs, "No idea. Now put this on, I need to make sure we have enough time for me to do your makeup. If the Bishop Brothers are going to be following you around all night the least I can do is make them want you more than they already do."

"They don't want me. They want to ruin my life. There's a difference."

She tosses a sundress at me, "Don't you remember back in school when they said boys only pick on girls that they like?"

"This isn't elementary school."

"No, you're right, we're adults, so the stakes are higher. They want you, Harlow, and I think you are playing into that."

Before I can think too much about what she is saying, my phone buzzes again in my pocket, too annoyed to let it go on, I finally take it out to see who is calling. I swear to god, if they don't stop tormenting me I'll be forced to do something drastic.

When I see my father's number lighting up the screen I almost gasp out loud. What the hell is he calling me for? Not once has he tried to talk to me since I left. Not once and now he's blowing up my phone?

"Which one of the three musketeers is it this time?" Shelby asks, while applying her foundation with a large makeup brush.

"Neither, it's my dad," I say.

She lifts a curious brow, "Wow, what could he possibly want?"

"Don't know, don't care." If there is one person I would enjoy talking to less than the Bishops, it's my dad. Pushing the decline button, I stare at the screen before powering it off. Whatever it is he has to say, I don't want to hear it.

Despite my better judgment, I let Shelby talk me into a short dress, at least it's not a mini skirt. I know I shouldn't play with fire, but after our conversation earlier the wheels in my head started to turn. Maybe if I made them as uncomfortable as they make me, they would back off a little? Then again, I don't know. Blurring the lines further doesn't seem like a good idea.

I pull at the bottom of the tight material as I sit down in Shelby's car, making sure I'm covered in all the important spots.

I'm not sure if the guys know that I left or that I'm headed to a party. They seem to keep tabs on me pretty well. Sometimes I even wonder if they planted a tracker on me. They're that good at knowing where I am and when.

"I'm so excited. Aren't you excited?" Shelby asks, and I swear she must have drunk two energy drinks and ate a pound of sugar before we left because there is no logical reason for her to be bouncing around in her seat with the smile she's wearing.

"A little, I guess." I shrug. I'm more nervous than anything. Mostly because I haven't been to another party since the night the brothers confronted me. I know it's going to be even worse tonight after all the rumors that have been spread about me.

"We'll have fun. Just don't let them get to you. Just like you said earlier, don't *let* them bother you. In fact, maybe you should find another guy, explore your options." I know she's right, but I can't help it. My track record with parties is horrendous. Every time I go somewhere it ends up being a disaster. The police get called, or I get pulled into dark rooms by brooding brothers.

The list goes on.

We get to the port a few minutes later to find the parking lot leading to the pier is already filling up. We quickly find a spot and get out of the car. The first thing I notice is that most cars on the lot have a Bayshore University permanent parking sticker on the back windshield. I was really hoping that there would be more people from out of town instead of the entire college.

The knot in my stomach grows, the pressure mounting when I see the girl from my building who called me out the other night.

This is a bad start to the night.

Seemingly unaware of my darkening mood, Shelby takes my hand and walks me down to the pier where the yacht is docked. Music is blaring from inside and lights are strung on the outside, illuminating the darkness. The yacht's already packed with people, their chatter meeting my ears.

"Oh my gosh, this is so pretty," Shelby gasps, her excitement infectious. I smile while we are crossing the little metal bridge onto the boat. My best friend's enthusiasm finally catches up with me and some of the tension starts to dissipate.

Stepping onto the shiny deck my wedges hardly make a sound. Shelby drags me across the deck following a string of lights leading to the party.

"What do you want to do first?" She inquires.

"Drink?" It's probably best to get some liquid courage in me before the brothers find out I'm here. Shelby tosses her blonde hair over her shoulder and starts to tug me in the direction of what looks like a bar, the entire thing lined with bottles, and cups.

"I thought you weren't going to come?" My body tenses at the gravelly voice behind me. With my hand still connected to Shelby's I spin around to face Banks. I'm about to spit out a snarky remark but whatever it was I was going to say gets stuck in my throat when I see him standing there. He looks like he's just stepped off a movie set.

My mouth waters, and the muscles in my belly tighten. He looks at me with the same heated gaze that I'm looking at him with, and I swear it's a good thing we're on the water because this entire thing might light on fire with these heated glares.

I drink him in. He's wearing a black button up shirt with the top button undone and tailored gray slacks. With one hand in his pocket, he looks like a fashion model striking a pose, and even worse it takes no effort at all. He's flawless looking without a single imperfection, and while I don't look bad either, I don't look like the other girls here.

"No, no," Shelby raises her finger towards Banks, "she is here with me, not you, so carry on and find someone else to harass."

"We'll see who I feel like harassing later on, for now, you are free to go," he says dismissively as if he has actual control over me. It takes everything inside me not to lash out, and make a scene. There's never been a time in my life where I've been in control. I thought college would be my chance, but it seems I lucked out, once again.

"Get lost, loverboy," she narrows her eyes, and snaps back pulling me towards the party. I don't even look back at him as we walk away, instead I let Shelby drag me through the crowd and straight to the bar. She pours two glasses of champagne and hands me one.

"Just forget about him," she says, as we clink our glasses together.

"Cheers," is all I say before downing the entire glass. I'm not much of a drinker but right now getting a little tipsy doesn't sound so bad. Maybe it'll help me stop thinking about men I have no business thinking about.

"Now we're getting somewhere," she smirks, filling my glass up once again. I don't chug this one but even just sipping on it, it's not going to last five minutes.

Shelby snatches a bottle from the bar, and we find a spot in the corner of the room. I've been on a yacht a time or two with my parents, but it was never like this. With so many people, and copious amounts of alcohol.

Looking into the crowd, I feel like every one of these people are having the time of their lives, all except me. I stop at one of those smiling faces, recognizing it. She sees me a moment after I spot her. Caroline's smile widens even more as she waves at me. I give her a half-hearted wave back, before I return my attention back to my drink.

Like a good friend, Shelby keeps refilling my glass every time it gets empty.

"I wonder how far out we are? We've been on the water for a while," Shelby questions. I just shrug. I don't care how far out we are, or what's going on around me. All I want is to enjoy the night and continue drinking my champagne in peace. The bubbly liquid makes the ache in my chest go away and replaces it with a fuzzy feeling.

"Speaking of water, I gotta go pee. Wanna come?"

"Nah, I'm good. I'd rather keep drinking."

"Okay, don't move, I'll be right back." I nod and watch her walk away, disappearing deeper into the yacht.

"Hey," a male voice calls out, followed by a light touch to my bare shoulder. I turn around a little too fast, losing my balance in the process, and end up landing in the guy's arms, well more like face planting into his chest, but it's the same thing I suppose.

"Oh, I'm so sorry," I apologize holding onto his forearms to steady myself. "I'm such a clutz." I blink up at the blond haired, blue eyed hunk holding onto me.

"It's okay," he laughs, and I notice the twinkle of amusement in his eyes, "I was going to ask you if you wanted to dance, but this is nice too."

The mystery boy smells like expensive cologne, and while he isn't one of the Bishop Brothers, he's handsome, nonetheless.

A nervous giggle escapes me and for a moment I forget why I didn't want to come here. This is fun, the drinking, mingling, and the quietness of the ocean around us.

"Dancing would be nice too," I try to say in a flirty voice, an actual smile pulling at my lips. The words come out slurred and I decide maybe it's time to lay off the champagne for a while.

"Thanks man, I got her from here," a familiar voice cuts in, accompanied by an arm being draped around my shoulders. I look sideways and glance up at Sullivan who is pulling me close to his side, away from the nice guy I'm talking to. His touch seems protective, but even I know better than to assume that's his motive.

He's up to something and it isn't good.

Still, I can't help but notice how delicious looking he is, like a piece of cheesecake just waiting to be devoured. He's wearing something similar to Banks, his shirt a striking red, which seems fitting since I want to make him bleed out right now.

Mystery boy pulls back, eyes wide, while lifting his hands. "Sorry, I didn't know she was here with someone."

"That's because I'm not," I grit out, shoving at

Sullivan's side which causes him to drop his arm. His lips turn up into a cruel smile, and to anyone else it would look as if he's on the verge of laughing but not to me. No, I can see the evil monster lurking underneath, waiting to come out and play.

He wants to hurt me, and even though I deserve it, it pains me that I can't just have one night to myself.

"It's not your fault, man, she likes to make me jealous by sleeping around. No hard feelings. I'll keep an eye on her for the rest of the night, make sure she doesn't suck some random guy off in the bathroom, *again*." Sullivan says dramatically. My mouth pops open, shock overtaking me.

What. The. Fuck?

The other guy's eyes grow wider, if at all possible, his cheeks turning crimson red, before he mutters a sorry and walks away. Once the poor guy is out of sight I turn towards Sullivan with my fists clenched, anger burning in my veins.

"Who the hell do you think you are?" I yell, shoving at his chest with both hands.

I expect him to say something, do something, anything, but instead he tips his head back and starts to laugh, and not just a normal laugh either. This is a belly shaking, laugh your face off laugh. If he wanted to embarrass me, to make me feel like dirt then he's succeeded, again.

"You're a piece of shit, Sullivan, and I wish that I never kissed you that night. I'm sorry for what happened, okay? I'm sorry, but this? This is too much. I don't care that I hurt you, nothing warrants this. Nothing." I growl and shove at him again. My little outburst is gathering attention, and I can already hear the whispers swirling around. Twisting around on my wedges, I start to walk away, but I make it less than a step before Sullivan's meaty paw lands on my shoulder halting me.

"We're done, when I say..." All logical thinking goes out the window, all I feel is rage, red hot rage and before I realize what I'm doing, my hand is moving through the air. Even over the music I can hear the loud slap of skin on skin as my palm makes contact with his cheek. Pain lances across my hand, but I don't care if I hurt him.

His words hurt me more than he could ever know. The blow causes him to take a step back, and out of the corner of my eye I see his gaze widen, his eyebrows lifting up to his hairline with shock. Like a fish gasping for air his mouth pops open. Lifting a hand to his cheek he touches the red mark left behind as if he can't believe that I actually slapped him.

There's a tightening in my chest, and it feels like my heart is breaking. Those blue eyes of his—that I've seen filled with compassion, and maybe even kindness in the past—fill with anger.

"Leave me alone. I'm done playing your games," I say feeling defeated, and this time when I turn to walk away, he lets me. My eyes are burning with unshed tears as I make my way through the crowded dance floor pushing anyone who doesn't move fast enough out of the way. I'm not sure my night can get any worse, and then it does.

Right before I walk out, I spot Oliver and Banks lounging on a leather sofa near the door. Each of them have a girl cuddled up beside them. I know it shouldn't bother me so much seeing them with other girls, hell, it shouldn't bother me at all, not after what just happened. But I can't help the sting of jealousy that lashes through me. It's like someone poured acid in my chest and I'm being painfully burned from the inside out.

They both look up as I approach. My chest heaves and I feel like I can't get enough air into my lungs. Oliver meets my eyes first, his smug smile turning into a frown but I don't know why. Before I can study his expression further, the long-legged blonde slides onto his lap and covers her lips with his.

Lips that I kissed only days ago. Lips that I can still feel on mine.

I clench my hands into tight fists and glance over at Banks, his eyebrows are drawn together almost as if he's concerned. It doesn't make sense, none of them really care. I've dug my own hole, and pushing them, letting them kiss me, touch me has just buried myself deeper. Unable to stand there and look at them a second longer I start walking out the door.

"That's right. Run along little girl," the bimbo on Banks' arm calls after me. I don't give her a second glance. She's not worth it. Not worth the anger. The pain. She deserves Banks. I just push out the door and into the cool September night. The tipsiness I felt moments ago completely vanished. The reality of it all hitting me is more sobering than a bucket full of ice water raining down on me.

Wrapping my arms around myself, I try and keep myself together in more ways than one. I don't want to be here right now, on this stupid boat. Feeling the panic inside me rise up I start walking around the deck, looking out into the vast darkness of the ocean. We are so far out I can't even see a single light past the water.

The wind is chilly and barely having anything on doesn't help to keep me warm one bit, but I would rather freeze to death out here than go back in there again.

Hopefully Shelby will notice that I'm missing and come out and find me soon.

Walking back to the far end of the yacht where I'm hidden by the darkness, I let go of the pain that's painting my insides. Tears start to fall down my cheeks, even though I told the bastards to stay inside. Placing my hands on the cold metal railing I let my head fall forward.

How did my life become so sad?

The question has been running through my mind for a while now. How did it come to this? Was is all my fault? My father's? Or maybe it was nobody's fault and we all just need to live with the cards we were dealt? Somehow, I don't think that.

One tear after the other cascades down my face, and into the dark blue ocean beneath me. All I want is for someone to hug me. To take me into their arms and tell me I'm going to be alright, that everything is going to be okay.

A brisk wind blows through my hair and I bite my lip to stifle the sob threatening to rip from my throat. I'm torn from my hug daydream by a hard shove from behind.

Everything unfolds so fast that I don't have even a second to react. One moment I'm standing by the railing, the next I'm being shoved over the edge, flying through the cold air.

A gut-wrenching scream rips from my chest, rushing past my lips a moment before my body hits the unforgiving sea.

Pain ripples through me on impact, petrifying my bones as a terrorizing darkness swallows me whole. Panic grabs onto every cell in my body, robbing my brain of any thought but one. *Survival.*

It takes everything inside me to push aside the feeling of a thousand needles prickling across my skin that the ice-cold water leaves me with. My lungs burn, begging, pleading for air. Squeezing my eyes shut I overcome the stiffness in my limbs and start kicking my legs with everything I have left to give.

I push and push, giving it my all, but if I've learned anything, it's that sometimes giving someone or something your all isn't enough.

CHAPTER SEVEN

My chest constricts the muscles so tight that I can barely breathe. I try and swallow but my throat, and lungs hurt so badly that it feels like an elephant is sat on my chest.

Somehow, I manage to get air into my lungs, though it feels like I'm breathing through a straw. Darkness still has a hold on me, its claws sinking deep into my subconscious refusing to let go, and let me open my eyes.

While I can't open my eyes, my ears still work. There are voices surrounding me, most of which I don't know. There is a gasp and a flurry of whispers that float around me like clouds wisping through the air.

Two voices stick out, reaching deep inside of me, making my shallow heartbeat, turn into a hard gallop.

"She's breathing," Oliver exclaims. I can hear him panting, attempting to catch his breath and I wonder what happened. There's a hand cradling face and somehow, I know it's his. I want to nuzzle into his touch, sink into his warmth, but I can't. I can't move at all. It feels like I'm floating just barely clinging to this world.

"Harlow, can you hear me?" Sullivan's voice caresses my ear. There's a pleading to his voice, telling me he's concerned, and I try my best to answer him, or at least, open my eyes, but I'm unable to do either. My lips part, my mouth opening, but words never come. All I get are my teeth chattering together.

Only now, with the touch of Oliver's hand do I realize how cold I am. More than cold, freezing.

"We need to get her dry and warm," Banks says, right next to me, two strong hands rubbing up and down my arm.

A second pair of strong arms slide underneath me and lift me into the air. My body curls in on itself as if out of instinct and my head falls against a firm shoulder.

"Everything's going to be okay. I've got you," Sullivan whispers into the shell of my ear while cradling me to his chest.

Strangely, that's all I need to hear to know it's going to be okay. He said he's got me, and for the first time, I believe him because I know, deep down, he won't let anything happen to me. In his arms I'm shielded, secure, and protected, at least for now. I let sleep pull me under once more. Even in the darkness I feel safe knowing he is holding me.

Awareness comes back to me slowly and the coldness that was threatening to eat at my limbs has vanished. My body still aches all over, but the freezing cold water has been replaced with something warm, something that smells delicious, and something that makes me melt into a puddle of mush. I try and stretch, but my muscles are stiff and tingling like I've been laying on them wrong. A pained moan escapes my lips as I try and move.

"Shit," I hear Sullivan's voice right by my ear. It's strained, and thick with restraint. "She's grinding her ass over my dick."

"I don't think she's doing it on purpose," Banks snickers.

"Tell that to my dick, asshole."

"Just think about something else," Oliver chimes in. "Or we can trade places, if this is too *hard* for you."

"Funny. I'm good right here. I'll deal with the blue balls later. You already did your part by jumping in to save her. When are we getting back to land and where the hell did Shelby go?" Sullivan growls.

Save me? Oliver saved me?

"Calm down. I sent her to get Harlow something warm to drink and to try and find her some dry clothes."

My eyes still feel impossibly heavy like there are boulders weighing them down, and now that the coldness has dissipated, I feel every single ache but intensified by twenty.

What happened to me?

"Why would she do that to herself? Have we really been that horrible to her? Is death easier than us?"

For a moment I'm confused. What are they talking about? I didn't hurt myself. I would never do that. Much like the waves cresting against a beach, pushing and pulling the sand my memories start to resurface in my mind.

Slapping Sullivan.

Walking out.

Crying.

Someone shoving me off the boat and into the water.

Oh my god. I almost died.

"I don't know, Sullivan, maybe we've been miscalculating this whole thing. She looked really bad when she was running out of there," Banks tells him.

"If you ask me, we've been kinder to her than her family's ever been to us." Sullivan says, this time. "But I don't know, maybe you're right. Maybe we've taken things too far."

"Stop. We don't know anything yet, not until she wakes up." Oliver says, in a low voice, a voice that says his word is final.

Digging deep I find the strength to pry my eyes open. It takes what seems like hours to do but can't be more than a minute. I blink a few times, my surroundings come into view. We're still on the boat that much I can tell from the slight bobbing motion, but we're in what looks like one of the cabins below deck.

The room is small and with all three brothers inside it, it seems even smaller. Banks is sitting on a chair to the left of me, and Oliver is sitting on the edge of the bed. A throat clears and I lift my head just the slightest, finding that I'm lying on a bed with Sullivan spooning me, both his arms wrapped tightly around me. Wiggling a tiny bit I feel soft fabric against my bare skin.

Naked? I'm naked.

As if he can read the horror on my face Banks says, "We had to undress you. We didn't touch, and we didn't look expect for when we had to, I promise." The wink he gives me is one that I'm sure is to ease the tension, but it doesn't.

"Yeah, you were freezing, your lips blue, and your skin ashen." Oliver says, and my gaze swings to him. I can see the pain in his deep brown eyes, but I don't understand it. I don't know why they care if I live or die? They certainly didn't care earlier with those chicks on their arms. My eyes fall closed for a moment as I try and gather my thoughts. I can't think about any of that right now. I almost died, someone pushed me off the boat.

"I... I didn't jump." I croak, my throat feeling raw, my voice sounding like someone else's and not my own.

"We're just glad you're okay." Banks whispers, his voice thick like honey. Weakly I turn my head and glance at him, the blue of his eyes blaze with anger, and sadness, the two emotions swirling together, bleeding into each other.

"Someone pushed me... I don't know..." My voice cracks again, and pain fills my chest. Who would push me? Who hates me enough to want me dead?

Before all of this, I would have thought they did? But then why would they save me? It makes zero sense.

"Shhh, we can talk about this later." Sullivan soothes. I want to tell him I'll talk about it now but I'm too exhausted to care, or to fight back. I let the warmth of his body heat encompass me. It wraps around me like a blanket holding all my broken pieces together. Slowly I breathe him in, he smells like rain, and citrus, it soothes the ache forming in my chest.

Closing my eyes again, it doesn't take long for sleep to drag me back down. It's a lighter, more carefree sleep this time. As if I'm just taking a little afternoon nap instead of recovering from almost drowning.

The next time I come to, I am being carried off the boat. I can't even move my arms because my whole body is swaddled in a blanket. Blinking my eyes open, I squint up and find that Banks is the one carrying me this time. I stare up at him for a long moment, taking in his features. I know it's stupid and that I have other, much bigger things to worry about but I kind of want to kiss him. Just to see if all of this is real, if I really did almost die, if they really did save me.

"Where do you think you're taking her?" Shelby squeaks. She sounds out of breath, like she's been running or something.

"We need to get her to the hospital," Banks snarls, his tone razor sharp.

His response pulls me from my dreamlike state and I start to panic.

"No," I croak. "No hospital." His pace slows when he hears my voice, concern etched into his handsome features.

"Please, I just want to go home and go to sleep," I plead. The last thing I need is to go to the hospital because then my father will be called, and I'd much rather die than deal with him right now.

Eventually Banks stops walking all together his gaze flicking around. When I follow his gaze I find Sullivan, Oliver, and Shelby all standing around us.

"I told you she wouldn't want to go. She hates hospitals," Shelby says, all matter of factly, her arms crossed over her chest.

"Are you sure?" Sullivan asks, looking at me, his eyebrows pinched together as he examines my face, like it's hiding all my secrets.

"I promise. I'm fine. I feel better already. Nothing a little soup, and sleep can't fix."

The guys exchange a look, what this look is, I don't know. I can't even really explain it. It's like they're agreeing on something without even speaking.

All three of them nod their heads and then Sullivan speaks, "Fine, but you're coming with us."

"What?" Shelby practically screams.

"She's coming with us, at least until she's feeling better," Sullivan announces, which only seems to peeve

Shelby off further.

"Wait, you're telling me that you're going to take her back to your house? You guys? The same people who hate her?"

"We don't hate her." Banks interjects.

"Pfft, could've fooled me, it was probably one of you that pushed her off the boat."

The statement is a bold one, and whatever response Shelby was trying to get out of them she earns because Oliver takes a menacing step towards her, his finger pointed at her.

"Oh yeah, because I'm going to shove her off the fucking boat, and risk my life jumping into the same waters to save her, for what? Fun?" Oliver's face twists, morphing into something I've never seen before.

Shelby snarls, "I don't know, maybe? It seems like all of this is a game to you guys. Who's to say you don't want her dead? Or maybe you just want to play the hero?"

A cruel bubble of laughter pushes past Oliver's lips, "If we wanted her dead, she'd be dead already."

Okay, so I felt that one right in the heart.

"Enough you two." Sullivan barks, "It's already been decided. She's coming with us." He turns toward Shelby who is rolling her eyes.

"You don't own her. Nothing has been decided at all. I'll take care of her." She argues, and I swear I see her stomp her foot in anger.

"Shelby, it's okay. I'll just go with them."

"Fine," she finally huffs. "But they better not hurt you," she gives all of them a stern look, one that says don't fuck with me or my friend.

"You okay?" Banks leans down, whispering into my ear.

Am I okay? Someone tried to kill me. I don't know. I don't have the strength to fight with anyone right now. All I know is I don't want to go to the hospital and if that means I have to go with them, then I will.

"Can we just go?" His grip on me tightens and I can feel the tension in his muscles. He gives me a lopsided grin that would normally leave me feeling all fuzzy inside.

"Of course, Princess." He says and starts to walk again.

"Dude, where are you going?" Oliver's voice filters into my ears.

"To the house. If you guys want to stay and argue you can, but I'm taking our girl home. She needs a warm bath, rest, and something to eat."

"If anything happens to her, I'm coming for all three of you!" Shelby yells, somewhere off in the distance, but all I can focus on is Banks' words.

"I'm taking our girl home."

Our girl.

When we arrive at the mansion I'm alert enough to walk by myself, but Banks being overbearing insists on carrying me.

"You're not even wearing shoes," he points out and I look down at me feet, my toes wiggling freely. I guess he's right, still I don't want to be a damsel in distress. I may have almost died, but my legs still work.

Oliver walks ahead and unlocks the door for us. Walking inside, Sullivan switches on lights as we go. It's strange to be alone with all three of them, almost intimate, like we're in our own secret little world where we don't have to hate each other.

"Alright, I'm going to go and get out of these wet clothes and into the shower. I'll be out in a little bit," Oliver says, before disappearing up the stairs. As soon as he's out of sight I feel it, this strange tug at my heart. Like being away from him is losing a piece of my soul.

Something clicks in my brain then. He saved my life. He jumped into the ocean in the middle of the night and somehow found me, pulling me out.

Thinking it once doesn't quite hit home, so I let it run through my head again.

He saved my life.

Oliver saved my life. My mind is still reeling from this revelation as Banks and Sullivan take me upstairs and into the bathroom attached to one of the guest bedrooms.

I watch Sullivan turn on the water and pour some bath soap into it, while Banks sits down on the edge of the tub, still cradling me to his chest, wrapped up in a blanket like a newborn baby. I watch the water fall into the huge corner tub, the bubbles building little cloud like mountains as it fills up. When it's about half way full, Banks starts to peel the blanket back.

"What are you doing?" I gasp, grabbing onto the blanket like it's my protective barrier. I kinda guess it is since it's the only thing shielding me from their eyes.

"You gonna take a bath with the blanket around you?" Banks asks, his thick brow raised curiously.

Shaking my head, I feel my cheeks start to heat. "No. I can take a bath on my own though."

Banks exchanges a disbelieving look with Sullivan before shaking his head. "I don't think you should be alone right now."

Clenching my jaw, I say, "I told you. I didn't try to kill myself. Someone pushed me. I'm not making this up. I swear. Someone pushed me right over the edge. One minute I was standing there and the next I was in the water."

"Did you see who it was?" Sullivan asks, his gaze colliding with Banks'. It's almost like they're communicating in some strange brother way, and whatever they're thinking or saying they don't want me to know.

Even stranger is Sullivan's reaction, it's like he believes me.

"No. I was holding onto the railing looking out onto the water and someone just shoved me from behind. I didn't hear or see anyone coming."

Remembering it makes me shiver. Who would want to hurt me? No one other than the Bishops, but the brothers didn't do it, they saved me.

"Either way, you almost died tonight, you shouldn't be alone right now. Let me help you into the tub and then we'll just sit down on the floor to keep you company."

Biting my bottom lip, I contemplate it. I guess they've already seen me naked, Sullivan was holding me under the blanket, and I let him feel me up the other night, so there is really no reason to be shy now.

"Okay, but don't look...I mean, at me... again," I say suddenly feeling self-conscious. I'm not anything spectacular to look at, nothing like the girls they were with tonight. My hips flare out, and my thighs are a little thick, my boobs are pretty stellar or at least I've been told. I'm short, with hair the color of sunshine but I'm nothing special and yet, Banks and Sullivan are staring at me like

I am.

Banks helps me stand up and frees me from the blanket. My cheeks feel like they are on fire as soon as the fabric is pulled away. As promised neither of them look directly at me as I step into the bath on shaky legs. Never in my life did I think I would be in this situation. The Bishop Brothers are supposed to be my enemies and yet here they are caring for me.

Banks places his hands on my arms to steady me until I'm submerged in the tub. The hot water soothes my sore muscles immediately and I sink down into the bubbly water with a soft moan.

"Your back is bruised a little bit. I can put some arnica cream on it when you get out if you want me to?" Sullivan asks, as he and Banks take a seat on the floor next to the tub. I'm not sure what arnica cream is, but anything that he wants to rub on me right now sounds good. My entire body is one big aching mess.

The water fills up until it's almost at the edge before Sullivan gets up and shuts it off. For a few minutes I just soak in the water and let the tension seep from my body.

"Do you want to call the police? If someone tried to kill you..." Sullivan suddenly breaks the silence.

"No," I cut him off. "I don't want to call the police. One, I don't have anything to tell them. I didn't see anything, plus I was drinking...*underage* drinking. I'm already the center of attention at school, there's no need to make things worse for myself. Maybe whoever pushed me didn't want to kill me. Maybe it was just a joke that went too far? I don't know but I don't want to do anything that might add to my problems."

"You really believe that?" *No,* but I want to believe

that that's all it was, because the alternative is too scary to consider.

"I don't know what to believe, but I do know that I want this to be over. I want to be a normal college student and forget this whole thing ever happened. I'm probably the laughing stock of the campus now." I frown staring down into the bubbly water. "Well, more than I was already."

"Look…" I glance up at Sullivan. Those blue orbs of his bleed into mine, making my heart skip a beat or five. I can almost see the apology forming on the tip of his tongue. I shake my head slightly, hoping he understands. I don't want an apology. I should be the one apologizing. All of this is my fault.

"You should stay here for a few days," Banks interrupts. "If someone really did push you, maybe it's not safe for you at the dorms anymore." Logically speaking he's not wrong, if it wasn't just some sick joke then that means someone's out to get me, but who?

"You don't really want me here, we all know it." I avert my gaze so they can't see the sadness flickering in my eyes. I'm ashamed over how weak I am for these men, how much I want them, when I know I shouldn't.

"If we didn't want you here we would tell you to leave, you should know that. I want you to stay, and although I can't speak for my brothers, I'm sure they feel the same."

"Feel the same about what?" Oliver says, walking into the bathroom, droplets of water clinging onto his hair. He looks clean and happy.

"Harlow staying here for now," Sullivan explains. "Banks thinks she shouldn't go back to the dorms if someone tried to kill her and I agree. It would make watching over her easier."

"Yeah, I agree too," Oliver says, without thinking about it. "It's settled, she stays." He decides clapping his hands together.

"Mhm, *she* is right here, and *she* should get a say in where *she* goes, right?" I say into the room, knowing damn well that they're all going to disagree with me.

"No." All three of them say at almost the same time. Each of their faces hold the same expression, a mix between *fight me*, and annoyance.

"Whatever." I roll my eyes and sink down a little deeper until I'm chin deep in the water. If they want to play hotel for the next few days, then so be it. It's not like they don't have the space here for an extra person and I'm not going to lie, this is much nicer than the dorm shower stalls. I allow myself to soak a little longer while all three of them stand and hover over me broodingly, like someone could possibly get to me in their guest bathroom. It's kind of cute how protective they're being. Almost enough to make me forget their bullying ways.

When it's time to get out of the bath it's just as awkward as it was getting in. The guys kind of avert their gazes but insist on helping me out. Sullivan wraps me up in a large fluffy towel and before I can take a single step he bends to pick me up. I don't even say anything knowing he's not going to put me down. What's the point in wasting my energy?

They want to treat me like fine china then I'll let them.

We walk back through the guest bedroom, but instead of putting me down on the bed like I expect him to, he keeps walking until we're in another room, a room that has to be his because it smells just like him. The room is vaguely familiar and I realize it's the same bedroom they cornered me in the night of the party. Except now the lights are on and I can see the contents of the room. Dark sheets, grey walls, a wrought iron bed, close to the floor. The room screams masculinity.

Reaching the bed Sullivan sits me down on the edge of it, and I sink deep into the memory foam mattress. It feels like heaven. I consider rolling over in the towel and letting the mattress swallow me whole when he walks over to his dresser and pulls out a shirt and pair of shorts. My eyes feel heavy and my muscles ache. It's starting to feel more like I fell down a flight of stairs and less like I was shoved off the side of a boat.

"You'll stay here tonight," he says, returning to the bed and placing the clothes beside me.

"I know, we discussed this already," I say midyawn. Our eyes meet and there is a warmness within his gaze that I've never seen there before.

"No, I mean *here*. You'll stay here, in my bed tonight. Tomorrow you'll stay with Banks and then Oliver. We'll switch off and on."

"Wait, what?" I tighten my hold on the towel, needing something to hold me to this reality because what he just said makes zero sense to me.

"Your dreams are coming true, Princess, you'll get to sleep with each of the Bishop Brothers," Banks teases from the doorway and I give him a disgruntled look.

Pfft, this is not my dream. Totally not my dream. I don't know what he's talking about.

"No. There has to be like three extra rooms in this house. I'll just take one of those. I don't need to be babysat while I'm sleeping."

Sullivan shakes his head, his features hardening as

he leans forward and into my face. I should shrink back, get up, run for the door, leave this house but I can't, not only that, but I don't really want to.

His big hand reaches out and cups my cheek and I bite my lip needing something to focus on so I don't nuzzle my face into his hand like an unwanted dog needing pets.

"Don't fight us, please, because you won't win. There are three of us and one of you. One way or another we'll get what we want. So let us do this for you. Let us take care of you. It's the least we can do."

The compassion in his voice tugs at my heartstrings. I must be having a mental break down because I'm on the verge of tears.

"Don't lie to me, we're enemies, rivals, you don't want me here," I whimper, my emotions breaking through the surface.

Sullivan smiles, really smiles and when he speaks, I swear my entire body breaks out into a shiver, "Rivals or not, I've always wanted you here." He pulls back, his hand dropping from my cheek, the moment ending all too soon. "Now, let's get you to bed. We can figure stuff out tomorrow."

Nodding my head I try to understand the feelings coursing through me. They should hate me, and they do, but there's something else there. The feeling is like a snake bite, the wound festering, the venom spreading through my veins. I look up from the floor and find all three of them staring at me. I've never felt so confused and complete all at once.

This makes zero sense but I'm too exhausted to try and figure it out right now. Maybe I'm so tired that I'm making this all up in my head. I should just go to sleep and reevaluate this whole day tomorrow.

And that's exactly what I do. I quickly slip into the clothes Sullivan laid out for me with the guys turning around like the gentlemen they are. I cuddle up on the king size bed, Sullivan stripping down to his boxers and crawling into bed next to me.

I gulp down the nervous anxiety of having him so close to me while being damn near naked. Banks and Oliver say their goodnights and leave the room. Exhaustion starts to tug at me and I'm only vaguely aware of the door closing and Sullivan leaning over to whisper in my ear.

"Sleep tight, Harlow," his voice carrying me off into a dark slumber.

CHAPTER EIGHT

When I wake up it's not yet light outside, the sky through the shades casts a dark shadow inside the room. Slowly I turn, lifting my head to find Sullivan still asleep. He looks so at peace. A Greek statue, with hard edges, and well-defined muscles that makes my mouth water.

I'm mostly laying on top of him my leg draped over his, my arm wrapped around his middle, those perfectly shaped abs pressing against my skin, with my head resting on his firm chest. I don't remember falling asleep like this, but I'm not complaining about waking up in this position.

My cheek is hot where my skin is pressed up against his and when I try to move, I realize his arms are caging me in, holding me tightly to his side. I know I shouldn't, but I feel secure, and protected in his arms. I'm content, so content that I almost forget that I nearly died last night. The unpleasant thought sends a shiver down my spine and I nestle even deeper, like I'm trying to embed myself into his skin.

"Are you cold?" Sullivan's sleepy voice vibrates through me. It's husky, and strokes something deep in my belly. My feelings for him—hell for all three of them—are spiraling out of control.

"I'm fine," I whisper, my own voice raspy and my throat sore from swallowing all that ocean water yesterday.

"How is your back? Are you hurting anywhere?" He questions, his voice strong.

"Just sore, but I'll be fine. I'm stronger than I look," I tell him as he starts to gently rub his hands up and down my back. I bite my lip to stop myself from making any loud mewling noises.

"Let me see it. I forgot to put some cream on it last night. I can do that now," he offers, nudging me off of him. I scoot away and lay down on my stomach beside him. This is bad, but oh so good. He peels the blanket away and gently pulls the shirt I'm wearing up.

The cold air of the room kisses my bare skin and I hiss out through my teeth at the sensation.

"Don't move, I'm getting the cream." He orders and gets up from the bed. God, he's so bossy, it's almost infuriating. I don't watch him, instead I bury my heated cheeks into the mattress. His scent swirls around me, it's inside me, in my pores, swirling around my head. I'm supposed to hate him, but hate is the last thing I'm feeling right now.

He reappears a moment later with a tube in his hand. Sitting down next to me, he squeezes some onto his fingers and starts to lightly massage my back. His touch is gentle, and sensual at the same time. It sends small jolts of pleasure up my spine and then back down again, and into my core.

"Oh god, that feels good." I groan into the mattress without thought.

"I told you I could make you feel better," he whispers, his hot breath caressing my ear. I can almost see the smug look on his face, the glint of mischief in his eyes. It doesn't take long for me to turn into a pile of mush beneath his strong hands. His fingers trail across my skin, the cream he used penetrating deep into my muscles. He pulls away and I'm not sure what overcomes me, but I feel the need to apologize, to tell him that I'm sorry for ruining everything for him last year. I never should've listened to my father, believed his lies, not when he was far worse than the Bishops.

Pushing up off the mattress I settle onto my knees, the shirt falling back into place. When my gaze finds Sullivan's, I see the heat in his eyes. Instinctively my eyes drop down to his boxers, a sizeable tent having formed there.

Shit, he's huge, and hard as stone. I lift my gaze back to his face before I say something to embarrass myself.

"I... I just want to say sorry, for that night, for ruining..."

"Shhh," Sullivan reaches out, pulling me into his arms. My lips press into a firm line at his touch. The organ in my chest starts to pound and my chest rises and falls in an unsteady rhythm. With his hands on my hips he moves us back towards the headboard. I gasp as his stiff cock presses against my center. He must be able to feel the affect he has on me.

"I don't want to talk about the past, in fact I don't want to talk at all." Fingers ghost over my hips and I wiggle against him, enjoying his hardness against me. His grip tightens and he groans, and I swear to god it has to be the sexiest sound I've ever heard in my entire life.

Lifting my hands I place them on his shoulders and

lean in, my lips finding his full firm ones. The kiss is saturated with lust, with a primal need for something more and like two souls trying to find their place in each other we collide with a heat that could rival the sun. Sullivan's tongue slips past his bottom lip, and presses against mine begging for entry into my mouth. Without hesitation I part my lips and our tongues meet, stroking each other tenderly.

My hands move all on their own gliding over his strong shoulders, and down his firm chest, over his eight pack abs, and to his tapered waist, before moving back up again, until my fingers find purchase in the longer strands of his hair, in this light it's almost a rusty color that suits him.

Breathlessly, he pulls away, the blue of his eyes the color of a thunderstorm before it rains, his pupils dilated, "Fuck, Harlow, I want to kiss you everywhere, taste every inch of you."

His confession should frighten me being how inexperienced I am, but it doesn't it excites me, because I would love nothing more than to have his lips on my skin, his tongue stroking me in ways I could never imagine.

"Do you want that?" He questions, leaning in to press a kiss over my throbbing pulse. Pressing down on his cock I swivel my hips, the pleasure that zings through me is indescribable.

"Yes." I reply hoarsely feeling only a little timid when he pulls away and grabs the hem of the T-shirt I'm wearing, pulling it up and over my head. The shirt falls to the mattress beside us, and suddenly I'm sitting in his lap, my breasts exposed, and my cheeks feeling fifty shades of red. Instinctively, I lift my hands to cover my breasts but Sullivan isn't having it, he shakes his head, and grabs onto my wrists, bringing my hands back to his shoulders.

"You're beautiful, and you shouldn't hide that beauty."

He just called me beautiful. I soak in the words and sink my teeth into my bottom lip when he leans forward and sucks one of the stiff nipples into his mouth. His eyes drift closed, and he moans around the tip, the sound pulsing through me.

My pussy clenches around nothing but air, and I wish so badly that he would alleviate the ache forming there. Pulling away he releases my nipple with a loud pop and moves to give equal attention to the other one.

"You smell like sweet vanilla. You're intoxicating, and taste like freshly picked strawberries. Fuck, I could kiss you all day, and suck on these pretty pink nipples for hours." Goodness, his words aren't helping matters.

I can feel something building deep inside me, it mounts higher and higher as he sucks my nipple, swirling his tongue across the hardened peak while kneading my other breast, his thumb and forefinger rolling the hardened nub gently.

"I'm... that feels good, even better than the massage."

Pulling away he palms both breasts, his eyes flashing with barely restrained need and in this moment, I want him to snap. I want him to take me, give me the pleasure that I know he can. The pleasure that he'll give, if I ask.

"I need you..."

"Grind your pussy against my cock. I want to see what you look like when you fall apart." He croaks, and like a kid being told they can have dessert before dinner I press my pussy against his cock—our thin layer of clothes doing nothing to hide our arousal—taking whatever he will give me.

At first contact I gasp, my pussy throbbing, and heat spreading through my core. Maintaining pressure, I swivel my hips and smile when a deep moan passes his's lips.

"So pretty, so fucking pretty," he murmurs, looking up into my eyes, his fingers plucking my nipples with a steady rhythm. I let my body's reaction to him overtake me, and start humping him, finding the perfect angle that brings me just enough pressure to set me off.

My movements become wild, my hips moving faster and faster, as the pleasure rises higher, and holy hell, I wish there was less fabric between us right now.

"Come for me, Harlow, show me how much you want my cock and maybe next time I'll give it to you." The deepness of his voice, and the erotic words set me off, heat pools inside me and then like a firework I explode. My entire being quaking, my pulse pounding in my ears as my pussy clenches over and over again around nothing.

"Fuck…" Sullivan grits out, his fingers digging into my skin.

Sagging forward I fall onto Sullivan, my ear pressing against his chest, the sound of his own ragged heartbeat filling me with warmth.

"It's been a long time since I came in my fucking boxers, but you, Harlow, hold a power over me that is both frightening and exciting. But believe me, next time I come, it will be inside of you."

My eyes widen and I gulp, wondering when the

next time will be. My stomach is in knots, but the rest of my body is relaxed, a puddle of mush. I pull away, my mouth popping open with a question on my tongue, when the bedroom door opens and Banks walks in. I can't imagine what he's thinking as he takes us in, his face is a mask of unshown emotion and before either one of us can say anything he exits the room, closing the door behind him.

I turn back to face Sullivan bashfully and he brushes a few strands of hair from my face. I'm a fucking mess. I just humped one of the guys I'd been taught to hate for the first eighteen years of my life. The same guys who've spent countless hours bullying me and making my life miserable. So why does this feel so right, yet so wrong? Having Banks walk in on us, is leaving me with a whirlwind of emotions that I don't know how to deal with.

"We can't help it, all three of us want you. The question is, do you want all of us?"

And if that isn't the million-dollar question, I don't know what is.

Breakfast isn't as awkward as I expected it to be and Banks doesn't mention what he saw in Sullivan's room. Still, this feels anything but normal. Part of me is still wondering if this is real at all. How can we go from hating each other to enjoying breakfast after cuddling all night? Then something dawns on me. Did we ever really hate each other? Or were we just conditioned? Did we just hate the versions of each other our parents made us see?

Looking back on it I can't really say I ever felt like I hated them myself, as in, they never did anything to hurt me directly. Everything I ever heard about the Bishops came from my father and now that I know my father lied to me I can't help but wonder if he lied about other things too. My mother never spoke of them, but when she did it was with the same disdain my father had.

Thinking about my parents always leaves a bitter taste in my mouth. I take a sip of coffee and try to wash down the unwanted memories. Instead of dwelling on the past I look over at the three men sitting at the table with me. I've never seen them so relaxed and carefree.

"I'll be gone most of the day, but I'm sure Banks and Oliver can keep you busy," Sullivan says, in between bites of his bagel.

"Where are you going?" I ask out of curiosity, only after the words leave my mouth do I realize how nosy I'm being. I internally curse at how ridiculous the whole thing sounds, Jesus, Harlow, he gave you an orgasm, not a wedding ring.

"Just have to deal with some stuff," he looks over at me briefly, obviously not willing to share. I take the hint and don't ask him to elaborate. It's none of my business really.

He leaves right after finishing breakfast and I try to help Oliver and Banks clean up the kitchen, but Banks instructs me to stay seated which leaves me feeling weird and out of place.

"I should probably just go back to the dorms," I announce, feeling as if I might be intruding or something. "You really don't have to do this. You don't have to take care of me, watch over me. I don't need..."

"We already talked about this. You are staying here

until we figure out who pushed you off the boat." Oliver's voice holds a finality to it, like what he says goes, and I know once again I've been shot down. I frown and cast my eyes to the floor, crossing my arms over my chest. I'm still wearing Sullivan's shirt. No bra, of course, and his shorts, with, you guessed it, no panties.

Even with the clothing I have on I feel naked, and out of place.

"Why don't we watch a movie or something?" Banks suggests, clearly trying to lighten the mood. "We can spend the rest of the day on the couch, maybe order some takeout, lay around and be lazy."

"Actually, that does sound really nice," I smile. "But, I need to at least call Shelby and let her know I'm okay. I know her, and by now she's probably worried herself into a frenzy. She'll be waiting around all day for me to call or come home."

Banks claps his hands together, the sound echoing around the room loudly, "It's decided then, lazy couch day it is. Here, you call Shelby," he says, sliding his phone across the table towards me.

"I'm hopping in the shower."

"And I'm going to pick a movie. Return to the living room in ten minutes," Oliver demands, his gaze burning right through me. I can't place the emotion I see there, but I can't look away. It's like he has be in a trance. He slips from the kitchen a moment later and I feel like I can finally breathe.

What the hell was that? Whatever it was it was intense. With the phone in hand I dial one of the few numbers I know by heart.

Shelby answers on the second ring with a dramatic gasp, "Hello?"

"Hi, it's me. Just calling to say I'm alive."

"God, Harlow, I've been worried sick about you. I don't think you staying there is safe. I feel like a shitty friend to have let this happen. I should have called the police instead. God, please tell me they haven't hurt you. I swear I'll murder them. I know how to hide a body."

"What? No! Stop, Shelby. I'm fine." I assure her, but I can tell from the heavy breathing she's doing through the phone that she's on the verge of a meltdown.

"You almost died, Harlow. Do you have any idea what it felt like to see them pull you from the water like that? You do know you weren't breathing when they pulled you out, right?" For a moment I don't say anything. That explains the pain in my chest, I guess. Someone must have done CPR on me. I lick my lips, preparing myself to say something, to reassure her that I'm okay, but the words won't come. I didn't know that, and honestly, I'm not sure I wanted to know that. I don't want to be reminded of how close I was to never waking up, to never seeing Shelby, or the guys, again. Swallowing down the fear, and sadness bubbling up inside me I force myself to speak.

"It was a freak accident. Probably just a joke that went wrong. I promise, I'm fine," I say weakly, wishing I was strong enough to believe the words I'm saying. She sighs deeply into the phone and I know she doesn't believe me. She's known me long enough to know I'm not okay, but she also knows I'm not ready to talk about it.

"Fine, but call me if you need me and oh, I almost forgot. This chick came by our room this morning, asking if you were okay. Carole I think was her name."

"Caroline?"

"Yeah that's it, she said she was worried about you

last night and wanted to check up on you."

"That's sweet," I say, wondering how she knew what room I lived in.

"I'm going to the gallery for a few hours, but I'll have my phone on me, and I mean it. Anything, Harlow, even if you just want to talk."

"I swear, I will call if anything happens," I assure her. "Thank you for being an awesome friend, I love you."

"Yeah, yeah. I love you too, bestie. Talk later." I press the red end key on the phone and stand there for a moment, regaining my composure. I wasn't breathing? I literally could've died, I was so close to death, but Oliver saved me.

He saved me.

CHAPTER NINE

I f someone would have asked me two days ago how I was going to spend my Saturday, this would have been by far the furthest scenario from my mind. Banks, Oliver, and I are stretched out on the oversized sectional, each eating out of a box of Chinese takeout, while watching all the *Die Hard* movies.

We are already at the end of the second one and Sullivan still hasn't returned. I wonder where the hell he is, but I don't want to seem nosy, so I keep my mouth shut and enjoy this day without worrying.

"How is your back?" Banks asks, when the movie ends.

"It's better, that stuff Sullivan put on there really helped."

"Is that what you two were doing this morning?" he teases. "Maybe I can put some *cream* on you too."

Oh God. I don't know if it's the reminder of what I did with Sullivan, or the suggestive tone in Banks' voice, or maybe the way Oliver's smoldering eyes are burning into me right now, but something has my core tightening and moisture building between my legs.

"You're cute when you're blushing," Oliver says as

he sits up and leans over to me. "Let's see your back." He tugs on my shirt urging me to lift it up.

I scoot to the edge of the couch and lift my shirt up on my back. I don't plan on showing more skin than that, but when Oliver starts running his fingers slowly up my spine, I have this overwhelming need to take my shirt off all the way. I turn my head and look back over my shoulder just as Banks reaches out for me as well. His fingertips grazing over my ribs.

With both of them touching me at the same time my senses go into overdrive. Before I know what I'm doing, I pull my shirt off all the way and drop it onto the floor by my feet.

"Fuck yeah," Oliver exclaims. Grabbing me by the hips, he spins me around and pulls me onto his lap. I straddle him in nothing but a pair of thin shorts, the fabric already soaked at my crotch.

I can't hold back a moan when I feel his very hard cock pressing up against my clit. With his hands sprawled out on my thighs he grinds me over his length, but I really lose it when he takes one of my nipples into his mouth and swirls his tongue around the tight bud.

My head falls back as pure lust overcomes me. Suddenly I don't care about how wrong this is, all I can think about is their hands on me, their mouths, their tongues, their...*oh my god.* I can't believe this is happening. Am I going to lose my virginity during a threesome?

Oliver sucks on my puckered nipple and I lose my train of thought again.

"Don't be so greedy, brother," Banks growls from beside us and Oliver releases my nipple with a pop.

Banks smiles and cups one of my breasts before leaning down to take the other one into his mouth while

I'm still straddling Oliver. The wrongness of it all is so exhilarating. I had Sullivan this morning and now I'm with his brothers.

I busy my hands threading my fingers through tufts of soft brown hair while Banks swirls his tongue around my hardened nipple. The sensations they both stir inside me are maddening.

Suddenly he stops and pulls away gently. I whimper at the loss of contact, my head too dizzy with lust as I try to figure out if I've done something wrong.

"Lay across our legs," he orders, tugging at my shoulder. With shameful eagerness I oblige, readjusting my legs so I can lay across both their laps. My upper body is on Banks, while my ass is nestled against Oliver's hardened cock.

"You want us to make you feel good?" Oliver inquires, his voice heady, while running his hand up and down my inner thighs. My heart starts to beat rapidly desire pooling deep in my gut.

"Yes," I say breathlessly, my tongue darting out over my bottom lip to wet it.

"I want to touch you," Oliver purrs.

"You are touching me," I tease, even though I know exactly what he means.

Grinning he uses his hand to nudge my legs apart.

"I want to touch you here," he murmurs and lets his thumb ghost over my shorts covered pussy. Taking the hint, I spread my legs further for him. He takes the invitation and trails his fingers over the fabric before he dips his thumb into the waistband of my shorts and starts to pull them down.

I lift my hips to give him better access and then watch as he pulls the fabric down my legs slowly, ever so slowly, leaving me completely bare. My eyes dart between both of them as they look down at me like I'm an all you can eat buffet and they are two starving men who haven't eaten in weeks.

Banks cups my cheek and tilts my face towards him. Leaning down, he presses his lips to mine, this kiss consumes me, ripping the air from my lungs. I'm so overwhelmed by that kiss that it's hard for me to keep track of where Oliver's hands are.

Pleasure builds further when Banks' free hand finds my breast and he starts kneading the flesh. At the same time Oliver's hand moves between my thighs to cup my mound, his thumb finding my clit with ease.

"You want us to make you come?" Banks asks, his voice unnaturally deep as he pulls away just enough to speak.

With his thumb firmly on my clit Oliver moves a finger to my already drenched entrance. This is insane, we should stop, but I don't want to, I don't know if I could stop right now. The world could burn to the ground around me and I wouldn't care. All that matters is the scorching fire flickering in my belly.

"Yes, please," the words come out on a gasp because right as I'm speaking them, Oliver slides one of his thick digits into my slickness.

"Fuck, Banks, she's tight as hell." Oliver's voice is strained, the muscles in his neck tight. He looks like he's ready to explode.

"Mmm, so tight and ready for us," Banks murmurs against my lips, before deepening the kiss. Seconds later my nipple is being rolled between two fingers, my chest heaving. My body shudders with pleasure at the explorative hands of these two men.

I whimper the moisture between my legs growing, dripping now. I'm so wet, so ready, it's almost embarrassing. As if he can sense my discomfort and need for more, Oliver starts to move, his finger pumping in and out of me with shallow thrusts.

"Fuck, you're so beautiful, Harlow, your pussy's taking my brother's finger with so much ease. I can picture you with my cock stuffed inside."

Dear lord, my cheeks heat at the admission. Could I handle being taken by two of the Bishops? Even more so, would I want to be? I already know the answer to that question and as wrong as it might be, yes. I would want to be taken by them, together.

Banks is filthy, his words egging me on, pushing me closer and closer. My legs fall apart completely, my hips rising slightly with each shallow thrust, while Banks continues to pluck at my nipples, alternating between the two while whispering filthy thoughts in my ears.

"You're so greedy, so willing and ready for us," Oliver growls, adding a second finger. He pauses briefly, before moving again, giving me time to adjust to him. It's almost like he knows that I've never done this before.

I feel full, so full, and the pressure in my womb builds as Oliver does this strange thing where he crosses his fingers inside me, rubbing at the tender tissue at the top of my channel.

"Shit," I gasp, into Banks' mouth and arch my back, pushing my breasts further into his hands. I'm full on panting now, my body moving on its own, my hands reach around, trying to find something to do.

One ends up in Banks' hair, my fingers digging into his brown locks. My other hand grabs a fist full of Oliver's shirt, pulling him towards me, as I teeter on the edge of insanity between the two of them.

"That's right. Come for us. Come all over his fingers, gush that pretty pussy all over his hand," Banks whispers against my heated skin, coaxing the orgasm right out of me. My thighs quake and my muscles tighten, the pleasure blinding me as it zings through my being from head to toe. I feel my channel spasming around Oliver's fingers, gripping onto him, and refusing to let go. My teeth sink into my bottom lip to stop the scream of pleasure from escaping, but some spills out anyway, ripping from my throat and from somewhere deep inside me.

"Ahhhh...." The noise vibrates off the walls. I squeeze my eyes shut and enjoy the last wave of the orgasm as it ripples through me like little aftershocks. Slowly I float back down to earth like a leaf falling from a tree.

Seconds tick by and I squeeze my lids tighter wanting the moment to last forever, but as the euphoric pulses of pleasure leave me, I'm left wondering what happens next?

I've not only kissed all three of them. I've done sexual things with all of them too.

Where does that leave me? Sandwiched right in the middle? Blinking my eyes open the first person I see is Oliver. He withdraws his hand from between my thighs, and brings the two fingers, now dripping with my arousal to his lips.

He slips them into his mouth, his eyes drifting closed as he sucks. He takes his time, like he's sucking on a lollipop. He's tasting me, tasting my arousal, my come and I'll be damned if it isn't as hot as hell to watch.

"You taste divine. I can't wait to have those thighs of yours wrapped around my face, with my tongue in your pussy."

Using my arm to shield my face—which is most likely cherry red—I hide from him.

"Don't be ashamed, that was amazing." Oliver assures me, his eyes darkened with arousal.

"Fuck yeah, it was. That's going in my spank bank for next time," Banks chuckles, while gently smoothing his thumb across my forehead. My breathing returns to a semi normal pace. My heart on the other hand is still galloping out of my chest and I don't think it will return to a slower rhythm any time soon. Not with Banks and Oliver looking down at me like they're about to devour me all over again.

I can feel both of their cocks straining against my bare skin, and for a second I'm scared of what's to come next. I want to satisfy them both like they've just done for me, but can I?

Can I take both of them, at the same time?

Banks must see the worry flashing in my eyes because he starts to shake his head.

"You don't have to do anything," he assures me, while running his fingers through my hair. The feeling is, there is no way to describe it. It's like a massage but for your scalp.

"I want to, it's just…" The sound of a door opening and closing echoes through the house, followed by heavy footfalls heading towards us. *Sullivan.*

I know I've done nothing wrong, Sullivan and I aren't an item, but I still scramble off both their laps with my shirt in hand, grabbing my shorts off the floor. I tug the shirt on over my head, and it just clears my tits when Sullivan comes strolling into the living room. Stopping in the doorway, he takes in the scene with his eyebrows raised, like he is trying to solve a puzzle.

"What the hell is going on here?"

"Oh, with us?" Banks grins, leaning back against the couch with his hands behind his head. My eyes dart between Sullivan, Oliver, and Banks. Sullivan's got a dark look in his eyes, while Banks is grinning like a fool.

"Well? Someone better tell me what the hell you guys are doing?" Sullivan pauses, his gaze raking over me once, and then a second time, except this time his gaze lingers on my bare legs. I feel like I'm being inspected.

I try and look anywhere but at Sullivan or the other two but my gaze keeps catching on two hardened cocks straining against the fabric of shorts. Fuck, that looks like it hurts.

"Why are her shorts off?" Sullivan asks, and Banks bursts out laughing. The tone of Sullivan's voice is deep, protective, alpha-like and I wonder why? Is he trying to stake claim to me? It sounds that way.

"Oh, we were just putting some cream on her back, like you did this morning, remember?" Oliver teases, a thick brow lifted, and though his response is directed at Sullivan his eyes are boring into mine. I swear if my cheeks weren't already on fire, they would be now.

Sullivan's eyebrows draw together, and then his lips twitch before pulling into a smile, "I see you've made your choice then," he says, reminding me of the question he asked me earlier that morning.

Did I want all three brothers? *Hell yes.*

Could I handle them? I don't know.

Is this a horrible idea that will blow up in my face, *yes*. This is wrong and not just because they are supposed to be my enemies, because our families have hated each other for years. No, it's wrong because I'm falling for three men who bullied me, who I thought for sure hated me, but clearly didn't hate me enough.

And if things end badly, which I'm sure they will, I'm the one that will get her heart broken, not them.

Turning on the balls of my feet I walk out of the room. I need some space, to be somewhere where I'm not surrounded by them and their intoxicating scents. Somewhere I can breathe without having a Bishop stuck up my ass. I don't know what's happening anymore, all I know is that we aren't enemies anymore.

"Hey, wait, where are you going?" Sullivan asks, the sound of his feet pounding against the floor behind me tells me he's following me. *Great.*

"Can you give me something to wear? Like some sweatpants or something?" I ask, stopping in the middle of the hallway.

Sullivan reaches out for me, his hand is heavy on my shoulder as he turns me around to face him, and I let him because I'm weak. Weak for him, weak for all three of them.

"Yeah, sure, whatever you need." He responds. Keeping my eyes firmly on his chest I say, "Thanks," and go to turn around, but the hand on my shoulder tightens and my stomach starts to flutter for some stupid reason.

He leans in to me, and I lift my head, unable to resist the closeness of his body. My nostrils flare as I breathe him in. All I can smell is rain, the smell of a thunderstorm, "Are you okay?" That voice of his is soft, wrapping around me like a cashmere sweater.

Suddenly my throat, lips, it all feels dry. "Yeah." I say, the tone of my voice softer than I expected it to be, "It's just all a little much and everything is happening so fast. I mean, one day you hate me and the next you want me to..."

"Whoa, slow it down. I've always wanted you," he admits, for the second time. Peering up into his eyes I see nothing but honesty reflected back at me.

"Well, I didn't know that," I say, chewing on my bottom lip.

"Well, you do now. Come on, let's get you dressed," Sullivan says, taking my hand and leading me to his bedroom. I take a seat on the edge of the bed and watch him dig in the drawers of his dresser. He hands me a pair of sweatpants and socks which I put on right away.

Once I'm dressed I feel a little better, less exposed and more put together, but not safe. These men have the power to strip me bare with a single look.

"Tonight you'll be sleeping with Banks," he reminds me, and I swear I can sense a change in his demeanor. He runs a hand through his hair as if it's a nervous tick.

"Okay, if that's what you want." I murmur, coming to stand fully. Even though I wouldn't consider myself short the brothers still tower over me like giants.

"You aren't ready for what I want yet, but you will be, soon, so very soon." The seductiveness dripping from his words nearly has me ripping my clothes off again. Stupid hormones, stupid feelings. I have to stop thinking with my vagina.

There's this low chiming sound that resonates through the house. Sullivan's eyebrows furrow together in confusion. Did someone just ring the doorbell? At ten o'clock at night?

"Who the..." He grumbles, but doesn't finish his question, he just turns around and heads for what I assume is the front door.

He makes it about two steps into the hall before all hell breaks loose.

CHAPTER TEN

They say there is always a calm before the storm, but there was nothing calm about what was about to occur. Three distinct voices pierced the air all at once. All three of which I knew, but one that I haven't heard in months. Not since the day I left home.

No. It can't be.

Each of the voices are coated with venom as they carry through the house vibrating the walls angrily. Sullivan gets a running start but I'm not far behind him as we both bound down the hall and then the stairs towards Oliver and Banks. Panic creeps up my throat, and the closer that we get to the foyer the clearer the voices become.

Oliver, Banks, and my dad. They're arguing, words being thrown like punches through the air. "You have fucking balls coming here, after what you and your daughter did to my brother, my family." My hearts racing out of my chest, the worst thoughts possible taking place in the forefront of mind.

"Where is she?" *His* voice is like acid raining down on me.

No. No. No.

What the hell is he doing here?

My feet don't even touch the bottom step and my mother is on me, wrapping her slender arms around me, hugging me with all her might, and it seems as if she cares, as if she's worried.

"We're here now, you're safe," she says into my hair with a relieved sigh her arms tightening around me, squeezing the life out of me.

I'm so baffled by the whole situation that I almost forget to push my mother away, almost. I push her away with a gentle nudge, and she looks at me with a stunned expression like I'm supposed to welcome her with open arms. I couldn't care less about her feelings though. I look past her to meet Oliver's gaze. There is a fury stirring in his brown depths, eyes that just a short time ago had passion, lust, and need for me in them. But that's long gone now, I can tell before I even open my mouth to ask what's going on.

"Get the fuck out of my house and take your lying daughter with you!" Oliver demands, his entire body vibrating as he takes a step forward to stand toe to toe with my father.

Lying daughter? What the hell is going on?

Confused, I look between my father, my mother, Oliver, and Banks. My head feels like it's on a swivel.

"What…" is all I get out before Banks starts yelling at me.

"I can't believe we fell for your lies again. You're one hell of an actress, I'll give you that," his words drip with hate. The way his eyes rake over me with pure disgust leaves me feeling like a piece of garbage floating in the wind.

The knife of betrayal slices through my skin cutting me so deep I'm sure I'll never survive the injury. I haven't lied about anything, haven't done anything wrong.

Shaking my head, I swing my gaze to Sullivan, maybe he'll talk to me, try and figure this out, but I should know better. His confusion turns to hatred before my eyes. He won't let me explain. He is making up his own story in his mind, and in that story, I'm the bad guy.

I look at his face and take in his contorted features I know it's over. His expression will haunt me for a long time, maybe even forever.

Disappointment, despair and hate...so much hate, cloud his vision. No longer is he the man that gave me my first kiss, my first orgasm. Instead he's the vile nightmare my parents always made his family out to be.

"I..." I start but am cut off.

"Shut up! Shut the fuck up and get out! You Lockwoods are nothing but garbage, liars, and thieves." The words hurt, and my cheeks sting as if he's slapped me. I'm so stunned that I can't move. All I can do is stare back at him wondering if I will ever see the Sullivan I love again.

"I didn't..." Oliver takes a menacing step towards me and I take one backwards out of instinct, my body telling me to run. The look he's giving me right now frightens me to the core. But not just because of the disgust in it, but because of the hate and the unforgiving rage. He wants to hurt me, make me feel the betrayal he's feeling right now.

"Touch my daughter again and I will have the police on your asses faster than you can call your pathetic parents," my father sneers.

Someone grabs onto my hand and starts pulling me towards the door. My legs move, but only because it's walk or be dragged and as badly as I don't want to leave, I don't want to be dragged out of the house like some fool either. It's obvious I've already done enough wrong, there is no point in standing here, begging for forgiveness. Tears sting my eyes, my heart thunders in my chest, and my stomach clenches with anxiety over the unknown.

What is going on?

I almost trip on the way out the door but right myself at the last minute. I blink rapidly like that might wake me up from this nightmare. I can't help but flinch when the door behind us is slammed shut, the noise vibrating through me. I'm dumbfounded, completely at a loss as to what is going on. Why are my parents here? What did my father say to Oliver and Banks that made their opinion of me change so drastically?

My mom drags me across the driveway to their car, rocks dig into the bottoms of my sock covered feet, digging deep enough to cut through, but I don't feel the pain, if there is any. Nothing could hold a candle to the pain residing inside my chest. My father opens the back passenger door and my mom ushers me into the back seat. I'm broken, confused, a shell of myself.

They get into the front seats and we speed off down the driveway, gravel kicking up under the tires.

"The Bishops, Harlow? What were you thinking? Did you sleep with one of them? Oh god, please don't tell me you let one of them touch you." My mother whines, pure disgust in her tone. She hurls about ten more questions at me before I manage to find my voice, my thoughts swirling and panic rising.

"What the hell just happened?"

"We saved you from the biggest mistake of your

life," my father barks. "That's what happened." His blue eyes clash with mine in the rearview mirror.

"What did you tell them?" I'm shaking now, fire filling my veins. I should've known. I didn't hear the whole conversation but in that one-minute Sullivan and I were upstairs my parents had found a way to make the brothers hate me all over again.

"That we know they had something to do with you almost dying last night and that we have plenty of people who were on that boat willing to testify to it."

Oh, my fucking, god. "You let them think I set them up... again. Didn't you?"

Instead of answering my question, my dad asks his own. "What if they had something to do with it?"

No, they didn't, they couldn't. It wasn't the brothers.

"There is no way they did! None of the Bishops pushed me in. Oliver was the one who saved me. How do you even know about the boat?"

"It doesn't matter how we know. Did you really think we would let our only daughter go off on her own without watching over her?" My mother asks, and I suppose I shouldn't be surprised. I should've known better, known that someone would be watching me, reporting back to them with every little detail.

"Yes, you should have! I thought I made myself clear the night I left, that I don't want to see you again? If I wanted something to do with you I would have answered when you called me. I would've visited you over the summer." I can count on one hand the number of times I've yelled at either one of my parents, but tonight it feels like déjà vu. I yelled the night I left and I'm yelling now, with good reason. How fucking dare they show up here, spouting lies, and interfering with my life?

"Don't be so dramatic, you don't have to stick up for them anymore. I've spent my entire life fighting against that family and I refuse to let my daughter be corrupted by such evil bastards." My eyes bulge out of my head at my father's words.

"Evil? You are the evil ones," I grit through my clenched teeth. "Drop me off at the dorm and leave me the fuck alone!"

"Harlow, language," my father warns as if he holds some kind of hold over me still. This might have been the first time I ever cussed at my parents, but I couldn't care less. I'm so angry with them. I didn't think I could hate them any more than I do, but once again they've proven me wrong. They've ruined everything by showing up here, everything.

"I hate you," I mutter, crossing my arms over my chest. It feels like my heart is breaking. I might sound like a hormonal teenage girl who is having a bad day, but I actually mean it. I hate my parents. I hate them for how they've raised me. I hate them for deceiving me, for not letting me be who I want to be and for destroying everything I love.

They took my image of people and distorted it. They twisted me, molded me into the person they wanted me to be. My entire world is crumbling, and I can't manage to pick up the pieces fast enough. I feel like I'm speeding down a hill in a car without breaks. What am I going to do besides crash?

"Swear to me, Shelby, swear it wasn't you," I beg, looking deep into her eyes.

"I swear, Harlow. It wasn't me! I haven't seen or talked to your parents since before graduation. I promise, I didn't tell them anything." I watch her face closely and find nothing but sincerity. My shoulders sag in defeat. *It wasn't, Shelby.* I've known her long enough to pick out a lie and she isn't lying, but if it wasn't her, then who was it?

Holding my head in my hands I say, "I'm sorry. I shouldn't have accused you. It's just my parents can be very manipulative. They could have you doing their dirty work without you even knowing it."

"I know, and don't feel bad you've been through a lot lately." She places her hand on my shoulder, and I lift my head. She gives me a weak smile. "So give me the deets did you send your parents packing?"

"I told them to leave me the hell alone or I would go to the police." I didn't want it to come to this. Even after everything, I hate that I actually threatened my parents, but I didn't see any other way of protecting myself.

I'd already moved hundreds of miles away, told them I never wanted to see them again and still they followed me, tried to control me, manipulate me. What else was I supposed to do to get away from them?

"Police?" Shelby asks, baffled.

"Remember when I told you how I overheard my parents talking about setting up the Bishops?"

"Yeah, of course."

"Well, I didn't tell you the whole story..."

It was already late and a school night, that's why I was sneaking down to the kitchen to get a snack. I was surprised when I heard voices coming from the living room because my parents usually went to bed early, but I didn't think too much of it until I heard a third voice that I didn't recognize.

"As always, it has been a pleasure doing business with you," a man spoke, his voice deep and there was a captivating darkness about his tone that had me stopping mid step.

"Likewise, Mr. Rossi," my father replied.

"I think we've been associates long enough for you to start calling me Xander," the man said.

"Very well, Xander," my mom purred. Followed by a girlish giggle. "Thank you again for helping us with the Bishop situation." My mom said their name as if it left a bad taste in her mouth.

"No problem at all, framing people is my second favorite work."

"Oh, what's your favorite?"

I can already tell the answer isn't one I want to hear.

"Killing people," the man confessed, without an ounce of sarcasm in his voice.

Nervous laughter bubbled from both of my parents' throats while bile rose in mine. I clasped my hand over my mouth and ran back up the stairs. I barely made it to my bathroom before vomiting out the contents of my stomach.

Once I was able to get up from the bathroom floor I went back into my room and opened the laptop. Xander Rossi was his name, I typed it in the search bar and hit enter. Immediately I had one article after the next pop up. Most of them were from the local news channel and newspapers.

Xander Rossi was the head of the local mob.

My parents had been doing business with the fucking mafia.

Shelby stares at me silently, and then her lips part, "The mob?" she finally asks, her tone filled with disbelief.

"Yes, *the* mob," I confirm. "That's when everything started going downhill. I confronted them the next day, I started digging, asking questions. Once I opened my eyes, I couldn't look away. All the lies, all the things I believed that they told me. I destroyed someone's life because of them, because of their lies."

I'm not looking for pity. I've taken responsibility for my actions, my parents on the other hand, have not.

"Wow, that's…wow," she says, her eyes wide.

"Yeah, so I'm done with them. I don't know what they were trying to do by showing up here and acting like nothing happened, but I shut them down."

"Good. You don't need that kind of negativity in your life," she says, and she is right, I don't need them in my life, nor do I need the Bishops. They were so quick to turn against me and didn't even let me explain. Which hurt like hell. They were too busy hating me to listen to my side of the story. I thought we had moved passed our differences, let the past go, but instead it feels like they were just waiting for a reason to turn on me.

They want to be enemies again. *Fine.* I don't need them, nor do I want them. They were pains anyway, or at least that's what I tell myself as I get ready for classes.

CHAPTER ELEVEN

I spend the next two days torn between wanting to reach out to the guys and trying my best to avoid them. Apparently, they're doing the latter, because neither Sullivan nor Banks showed up to the classes that we share.

Like the moping teenager I am, I walk to the local coffee shop in the afternoon, getting a hot cocoa and the biggest chocolate fudge brownie they have.

"For here or to go?" The girl with bright pink and purple hair from behind the counter asks.

"To go, please."

"Hey, Harlow," a familiar voice calls. I turn to find Caroline standing a few feet away. "Looks like you had the same idea as me," she smiles. "I'll have the second biggest brownie," she tells the barista.

"Hey, Caroline," I take in her warm smile. Shelby's been busy at the gallery and suddenly sitting down with a friend seems more appealing than sitting outside on a bench in the quad by myself.

"Want to sit and stuff our faces with sweet goodness together?" I ask.

"Sounds amazing,"

We pay, get our orders, and sit down in the corner of the coffee shop, near a bookshelf that's brimming with books.

"How have you been?" Caroline asks, as I shove a piece of brownie into my mouth. It tastes like Heaven and chocolate had a baby.

I shrug, "Okay."

"You really scared us all on the boat, the other night. When Oliver pulled you out of the water your lips were blue. I was worried you weren't going to make it."

"It really wasn't that big of a deal," I lie. It was a huge deal, someone had wanted to hurt me, who, I didn't know, but I also didn't want to worry Caroline with that admission either. I hope she doesn't ask me if I jumped.

I don't want people thinking I'm suicidal either, though I'm sure if I put my ear close enough to the ground within the gossip circles I'm sure I'll hear a rumor being spread about me.

She jumped, no one pushed her. She's crazy.

"Mhm, then why do you look like you're having the worst week of your life?"

"Well, I just have some personal stuff going on, and you know not to be weird, or anything, but every time I feel like I need a friend or someone to lift me up you appear like a fairy godmother."

A soft giggle escapes her pink lips. "That's me, the fairy godmother of friendship." Soft chatter surrounds us as we nibble on our brownies together. I wash mine down with even more sugary goodness, hoping that the sugar high will give me enough strength to get through the rest of my day. As badly as I don't want to admit it, the brothers have ruined me.

I've grown dependent on them. Where having

them around, and following me, annoyed me at first, I kind of grew accustomed to it and now that they aren't I just feel alone, discarded like trash. I'm sure that's the point though, to make me feel like shit.

"Are you sure you're okay?" Caroline asks again, placing a gentle hand on my shoulder, concern flickering in her eyes.

I look up from my brownie, "Would it be weird if I said I was in love with three guys?"

Caroline blinks, a neutral look on her heart shaped face, "It's 2019, who cares if you love three guys? Love is love, right?"

"Right, but..." I swallow my throat suddenly feeling dry. "What if they're three guys that you shouldn't want to be with? Like they're bad for you, but you can't help yourself?"

"Ooo, kinda like these brownies?" She says, wiggling her eyebrows, and popping another piece of gooey goodness into her mouth.

"Yes, kinda like these brownies."

"You indulge, I guess. I don't know, do what you think is right?"

I want to tell her I have no idea what is right or wrong, but I don't. I won't bore her with the details of my dramatic weekend. I don't want to send her running for the hills.

We finish our brownies, sneaking in a little small talk here and there. By the time we're finished my belly is full, and I'm back to smiling again.

"If you're still struggling with English, I can help you. We could meet up in the library or something one of these nights. Go over notes?"

"You would do that for me?" I ask, as we walk out of

the coffee shop and towards the quad where I will most likely end up seeing at least one of the Bishop Brothers. It's strange, because now that they're not following me around like lost puppies I find myself watching for them. I want to see them. Hell, I crave them, my belly tightens, heat blooming deep down inside me when I think of them.

"Of course, you've got a lot going on and what kind of friend would I be if I didn't offer to help you?"

"Honestly, a typical one. In case you haven't noticed I don't have many friends here." I mumble, wrapping my hand around the strap of my backpack. In the back pocket of my jeans my phone starts to vibrate. Laughter meets my ears, but I'm too busy unlocking my phone and looking through it to look up and see what has people laughing.

"Harlow..." I can hear the worry in Caroline's voice without even looking at her face to confirm it.

My phone continues to vibrate, and vibrate, and vibrate and I'm starting to get flustered with all the incoming text messages. Lifting my head my gaze catches on the east campus building where I notice a banner blowing in the wind. Bright pink lettering painted across the white canvas. *What the hell is that?*

Harlow Needs More Dick- Send Pics If you're DTF!

Below is my cell number, which explains all the incoming texts. The letters are so bright you couldn't miss them if you tried.

Joy. Another stunt from the Bishops. I should've known things would go from bad to worse.

"Like, oh my god, its Harlow the whore in the flesh," a girl sneers from a few feet away. I look up and see it's one of the groupies from the other night. The one that was crawling all over Oliver, or maybe it was Banks I don't remember, and I don't really care. Her name's Tiffany, that's all I know.

I tell myself to look away, to push my feelings down, swallow my pride, and turn the other cheek but I can't help myself. Like bile rising up my throat, the anger, and red-hot rage burns through me, and I find myself crossing the distance that separates us without thought.

"Did you do this?" I growl, pointing to the banner behind her.

She shrugs, purses her lips, and juts her hip out looking at me like I'm a peasant and she is the queen. To think that I used to be treated like a queen. If only she knew where I came from, the power I used to have, the power I no longer care to have.

"Maybe. Maybe not? Why's it matter? Last I heard if you can handle three you can handle them all." Laughter bubbles out of her, and the girl standing beside her. She looks familiar too, but my bone isn't with her, it's with her friend.

She thinks she's perfect with her platinum blonde hair, and painted on face, but she's just like the rest, a snotty bitch. My hands curl into fists, my nails digging into my palm.

"What are you going to do if I did?" She narrows her gaze and taunts me with a shit eating grin on her lips. I've endured enough bullshit. I came here to escape, to get away from the pain, the drama, but it seems it just followed me and I'm done, so done.

I react without thought pouncing on her like a cat. I pull back my fist and slug her in the face. Pain radiates up my arm while a scream that sounds like I'm murdering her pours from her lips. We scuffle across the grass, her fingers digging into my hair, pulling at the strands, causing a burning pain to flare across my scalp.

Bitch. I do the same, and when she starts to shriek like a pig, her arms flailing and her hands landing anywhere they can, I smile, feeling completely satisfied with myself.

"Harlow!" Caroline is grabbing onto my shoulders, and pulling me back, but not before I land another punch on the bitch's nose. Chest heaving, and heart racing I take a step back and look at the girl lying on the grass, droplets of blood dribbling down from one of her nostrils.

"You're trash. Nothing but a trashy whore," Tiffany snarls, shoving up off the grass. I smooth a hand over my hair and down the front of my jeans. By now a crowd has gathered around us, and I fully expect to be called into the dean's office for this little stunt. Whatever the punishment, it'll be worth it.

"I know what she did was wrong, but you can't just go around beating people up," Caroline scolds while shaking her head, sending strands of her dark hair across her panicked face. Shit, I know she's right but, god that felt good. Caroline starts pulling me away from the crowd and I follow her gladly, ready to get away from the gawking audience.

"Well, look who it is," a familiar voice hisses and it has me stopping mid step. "Can't get enough attention, can you?"

I turn and find Sullivan, Oliver, and Banks staring at me. Sullivan looks unimpressed with my little stunt. Banks has a stupid grin on his face that I would like to wipe off with my fist. And Oliver casts nothing but a cold glare my way. I know I should just walk away, I have already made the target on my back bigger by fighting

Tiffany like this.

Unfortunately, my anger gets the better of me and before I can get a grip on it, words are pouring out of my mouth.

"I hope you're happy," I spit at them. "I'm guessing you had something to do with this?" I point at the banner.

"It's not our fault that you're such a slut," Banks says, and I see red. Like a bull I charge him, pushing his chest so hard he stumbles back a few steps.

"You are just making this worse for yourself," Oliver sneers.

"All you had to do was let me explain!"

"We are done listening to your lies, Harlow. You made your bed, now it's time to lay in it," Sullivan growls, his voice sinister.

For a moment I just stand there looking at them, trying to see the men who kissed me just a few days ago, the guys who held me and made me feel safe. I search for that compassion deep in their eyes, but all I see now are guys who hate me and want to hurt me.

"Harlow, we should probably..." Caroline places a hand on my shoulder.

"Yes, we should," I whisper. We walk away from the crowd with me trying to ignore the nasty looks and condescending murmurs following me.

"It's going to be okay, Harlow," Caroline says, "We'll figure this out."

"I wish that was true." Oh god, I hope she is right. Is everything going to be okay? Can I figure this out? Or is this going to be my life from now on?

Caroline walks me to my dorm. She asks me repeatedly if I'm okay and I give her the same answer, "*yeah,*

I'm fine." She wanted to come up and watch a movie, probably thinking she would be able to take my mind off this whole thing, but I know there is no hope, so I send her home.

My room is empty when I walk through the door. Shelby is gone again and when the realization I am alone hits me, I break. I crumble to the floor like a rag doll, covering my face with my hands as I let it all out.

All I wanted was to escape but it seems I've traded one prison for another, the only difference is this time my heart is paying the price.

The next day goes just as badly, maybe even worse. I can't go anywhere without people looking at me like I'm a piece of shit. Sneers, laughter, and shitty remarks follow me wherever I go. Ignoring my surroundings is getting harder and harder to do.

I try to keep my head down and in one of my books, but my mind keeps wandering to the Bishops. I can't get over the way they looked at me. I'm so angry at them, for refusing to let me talk, for further embarrassing me in front of everyone, but I'm hurt at the same time. My heart a bleeding mess because for some reason I thought maybe they cared, that maybe they *loved* me.

Stupid, so stupid.

This all could've been avoided if they would've they just let me explain.

As I'm walking to my next class across the west side of campus, I notice two guys walking in my direction. Even though my gaze is on the ground I can still see two dimpled grins forming on their lips and I just know they are going to make a comment about me when they pass. Everyone else has, so I don't expect them to be any different.

Grabbing on to the strap of my backpack, I mentally prepare myself for the verbal assault that's to come, but as they pass neither says so much as one word. And it's then that I learn there are far worse things that can be done then spouting nonsense.

Instead one of them does something worse, he grabs my ass. The jerk grabs my ass, his meaty fingers sinking firmly into the fabric of my jeans. Then he squeezes, hard.

Yelping, I whirl around, my fists clenched, and nostrils flaring, "What the hell is wrong with you?" I grit out through my teeth.

"What? Not kinky enough for you? You need something better?" He grabs onto his junk and shakes it a little bit before releasing a chuckle into the air.

He moves away, following his friend who is a couple steps ahead, also smiling and laughing. *Assholes.* They're both lucky they walked away. I would've kicked their asses if I had to.

It's not until I make it to the classroom that I realize I'm shaking. I'm not sure if it's from anger alone or if I'm a little shook up from that guy grabbing me. My emotions are so out of control it's hard to pinpoint their origin.

Sinking down into the chair, I start to unpack my books and notepad. This is the class I normally have with Banks, but I don't expect him to show up. That's why I'm shocked when I look up and see him walking into the room.

Like magnets drawn to each other, his eyes find

mine immediately. For the shortest moment I think he is happy to see me, a smile ghosting his lips, then as if he remembers where we are, his face turns to stone. With a mask carefully placed over his features, he walks in and takes a seat two rows in front of me. My heart starts to beat wildly, my throat tightening, and my chest aching.

Seeing him is torture, especially right now when all I want to do is run up to him and bury my face in his chest and inhale his sweet scent. I feel weak for needing him and it feels so wrong that I still want him like I do.

Taking a deep breath, I try to shake the unwanted thought away. Just when I get my heart rate back under control, and my chest stops heaving, someone else walks in. *Tiffany*. Shit, I forgot she was in this class too. Guess I should think about who I share classes with before I decide to throw down with them.

She lifts up her nose and struts through the room like it's her own personal runway, and I hope someone would put a foot out so I can watch her tumble to the ground. Naturally she takes the seat beside Banks, who of course puts his arm across the back of the chair. Exhaling I grit my teeth together.

I tell myself it doesn't matter, she doesn't, he doesn't, but that would be so much easier if I could actually believe what I'm telling myself. Peering at me over her shoulder, she gives me a smug smile, like she won something, and I can't help but appreciate the way her smile is a bit uneven. She might have been able to cover up the blue and black skin with makeup, but she can't cover up that her cheek is still swollen from where I punched her. I had expected to get into some kind of trouble, but it never happened.

I don't know if that's because of the Bishops or if

Tiffany's just worried that I'll kick her ass again if she says something.

"Stop staring," she scoffs.

"Stop looking so hideous," I respond, crossing my arms over my chest. She already thinks I'm a bitch and I'd rather be seen as that than a push over. I've laid down, took the hate, let the Bishops bully me, but I'm done.

I don't want their hate anymore. I want something else.

"Awe, is Harlow jealous?" Banks chimes in, twisting around in his seat. My entire body lights up, ripples of electricity dance across my skin at the deep baritone of his voice. The coldness in his blue eyes reminds me of the ocean the night that I fell off the boat, cold, and unforgiving. Lifeless and impossibly deep.

"Not jealous," I lie, because let's be honest, I am jealous. "Mostly angry, but also, I feel sorry for you, that you had to stoop so low and hook up with someone like this," I lift my chin to Tiffany. "It's sad that you're trying to replace me, as if she ever could, but whatever, she can have my sloppy seconds."

Those cold depths of his flicker with fire, and his chiseled jaw turns to stone, he looks like he wants to snap me in two and knowing that makes me sit up a little straighter in my chair. It makes me a little happier, knowing that I still have some type of hold on him, even if it's not the kind I'm really after.

"Watch it, Harlow, my brothers and I can bring you great pleasure, but we can also bring you great pain."

He doesn't give me a chance to respond, the professor walks in a second later, and Banks turns around in his chair to face the front of the class. But I don't miss the warning in his voice. He wants to scare me, but the only thing that scares me is losing my chance with them.

CHAPTER TWELVE

The alarm on my phone goes off, the annoying ringing letting me know my laundry is dry. Putting my kindle down, I grab my spoon and chuck it into the sink and put the ice cream tub back into the freezer. Most people my age are out partying on a Friday night, but me, I would much rather be reading, and chilling out in the dorm. It would be nice if Shelby was here, but they have some really important artist coming to town, so she's stuck working at the art studio all weekend. It's whatever though, as long as she is happy, then I'll be happy for her.

I leave my dorm and head downstairs, my slipper covered feet making hardly any noise against the steps as I head outside to the side building. It houses the student laundry. If my mom ever found out I was doing my own laundry she would be appalled. I didn't wash my first load until a few weeks ago, and even though it was kind of a nightmare at first, for both Shelby and me. I'm proud to say that I've kept the accidental dye jobs and bleach spots to a minimum.

Its past ten and most students are out partying, which leaves the dorm area quiet and empty. I make my way around the building in the darkness of the night. Only two street lights illuminate the sidewalk as I hurry around the building. I'm probably imagining it, but I have this weird feeling that someone is watching me. Like a sixth sense, the hairs on the back of my neck stand up as a shiver runs over me.

The feeling doesn't ease up, even when I finally walk into the communal laundry room that holds about ten washers and ten dryers. The space is completely empty, silent. It almost seems deserted.

Scurrying across the room I grab my basket off the top of the dryer and set it on the floor.
I open the dryer and start grabbing my clothes, stuffing them into the basket without folding them, because who the hell has time to fold. It isn't until I grab the second handful that I notice something black on one of my white T-shirts.

Plucking the T-shirt from the basket I lift the fabric and stare at the front of the shirt in horror. Written there in large black block letters is the word **SLUT**. What the fuck? Shaking my head in disbelief, that someone would even be that immature I pull out another handful of clothes. I pray that's the end of the cruelty, but I should know better. One of my favorite sweaters has been destroyed. I cringe when I see the word **WHORE** written into the pink fabric, streaks of black ink bleed into the shirt and I know I'll have to toss it out. I know it's just a shirt, but it's mine, it belonged to me.

One by one I check every piece of clothing. Every single one has something written on it, something horrible, and offensive, and something that doesn't represent me as a person at all. But the person who wrote these hateful words wouldn't know that, because they believe only what they want to.

Angry with the world I stuff all the clothes into the basket and slam the dryer door shut. The sound so loud it echoes through the vacant space. My hands are shaking as I grab the basket and place it against my hip to carry it. I will myself not to cry, but the tears well in my eyes anyway. College wasn't supposed to be this bad, high school totally, but college? People were supposed to act like adults, be mature, make good choices, and stick up for others. I guess I never expected the brothers to follow me. That threw a wrench into my perfect future.

They wanted revenge, well, they had gotten it and the next time I see them I was going to tell them that. I'm going to let them see how broken I am. I deserved the pain, the hate, the anger the first time around, but this? No. Enough is enough. My parents showing up wasn't my fault, someone set me up, just like with the boat, and if they would've listened maybe things would be different.

With my laundry basket of destroyed clothes in hand, I speed walk back to my dorm. My vision is blurry with unshed tears that I try to blink away. There's a tingling on the back of my neck, it's the same feeling I got earlier.

Someone is watching me. What if it's the same person who shoved me off the boat? Panic claws at me and I take the corner a smidge too fast, catching the edge of the basket on the wall. The impact sends the basket to the ground knocking it out of my hands. Clothes spill out on the sidewalk and into a big pile of textiles.

Fuck my life.

I'm tempted to just leave them and run back to my room but decide not to give someone the satisfaction of seeing them sprawled out across the concrete. The last thing I need is my panties strung up like lights across campus. Angrily I bend down to grab the last shirt off the concrete, my fingers brush against the fabric when I get this strange feeling in my gut, like something bad is about to happen. I have this sudden urge to scream, and so I do.

A blood curdling scream rips from my throat just as a large figure appears next to me. I scramble backwards, landing on my ass, pain flaring across both cheeks as the figure crouches down next to me. His large hand reaches for me and if I hadn't recognized the face attached to that hand, I would have probably suffered from a heart attack.

"Calm down," Oliver's deep voice pricks my ears, his eyes scanning my face. Can he see the tears, the sadness in my eyes? "What's wrong with you? You look like someone kicked your dog and pissed in your cheerios."

"What's wrong with *me*? What's wrong with *you*? Actually, what's wrong with all of you? Have you been watching me, again? I can feel eyes on me."

"Stop, no one has been watching you." He says it like I'm crazy for thinking it, and hell, maybe I am, maybe it's all in my head.

Picking up the basket and its content, I get back up onto my feet. Oliver reaches for something on the ground and to my embarrassment it turns out to be a pair of my panties. Sadness overrules my anger and humiliation. I'm sad because having Oliver this close after everything is hard. So hard. I hate not being able to fall into his embrace and feel protected. Instead, he's standing there holding my panties that have the word CUNT written on them.

I try my very best not to cry, but my best is not

good enough today, my only hope is that the light from the building is not efficient enough to show my tears. Snatching the piece of cotton from his hands I start walking away from him, but to my utter surprise he grabs my wrist and pulls me back towards him.

"What's wrong?" he asks again, his voice softer and I can't help but burst into laughter. It's not a 'ha ha that's funny laugh', it's a humorless, sad laugh with a sob in between.

"Did you seriously just ask me that?" I'm surprised by the question, but I'm even more surprised when he takes his hands and cups my cheeks, he drags his thumb over the delicate skin under my eyes and wipes the last few escaping tears away.

And like a river with overflowing banks the words flow freely past my lips.

"You want to know what's wrong? I want you, I want all three of you, even after everything, I want you, and trust me, I know I shouldn't, I know it's wrong and it will never, ever work, and I know you're back to hating me. But, at least I admit how I feel." A moment of silence settles between us as he lets the words sink in while continuing to stroke my cheeks with such softness it takes everything in me not to sink into his touch.

I can see the turmoil in his chocolate gaze, "You're right, it won't work and it's all kinds of wrong..." I wait for the unspoken but, but it never comes. I don't miss the pain and want in his eyes though. I'm too familiar with both not to notice it. "We all want something that we can never have, and you, Harlow, are the one thing my brothers and I can never have."

I swear my heart breaks a little more inside my chest when he leans forward and presses a soft kiss to my temple. His lips burn into my skin and my whole body starts to tremble.

When he starts to pull away, I say, "I didn't call them, my parents. I don't know who did, but I didn't, and I didn't tell them that it was you or your brothers that pushed me off that boat. Someone set me up."

Oliver nods, taking a step back, while exhaling a breath. He looks so conflicted when he says, "It doesn't change anything. We were born rivals and we'll remain rivals. Your family's damaged mine and I can't betray my parents by loving the enemy."

Love? I watch his Adam's apple bob up and down as he swallows. He turns to walk away, and I anchor my feet into the ground to stop myself from going after him.

"You love me?" I croak, unable to stop the question coming out.

Oliver blinks, his long lashes fanning against his cheek, "Don't waste your love on somebody who doesn't value it," he says before giving me his toned back and walking away. He's speaking in riddles, does he mean I don't value his love? Or they don't value mine?

My head is a cluster fuck, my emotions sprawled out across the concrete like my clothes were a short while ago. Someone is out to hurt me, to destroy me and I can't tell if it's the three men I'm falling for or someone else.

I turn and take one step before I come to a sudden halt yet again. Standing a few feet away from me with her arms crossed over her chest is Shelby.

"What the hell are you doing, Harlow? Haven't they done enough?" She scolds me.

"It's complicated, I..." I start but can't come up with any further explanation. "You don't understand."

"You're perfectly right, I don't understand. I don't understand how you can be so naive and keep letting them play you like this. Haven't they proven over and over again that they are out to get you? They don't love you, they don't even like you. You let them do this to you, you *let them* break you and then I'm the one you go to in order to pick up the pieces."

Her words slice into me like a dull knife. They hurt incredibly bad, especially because on some level I know she is right. I let them close, I let them touch me and kiss me, because I wanted them to, no matter the consequences. They wanted to hurt me, and I let them, but the way Oliver just looked at me, the words he spoke. He said love, he said he loved me and deep in my heart I feel that he wasn't lying. He loves me and I love him.

"I'm sorry you feel that way, Shelby. But I can't help the way I feel, and I think deep down they feel the same about me."

"Then you are stupid. They don't care about you and I'm done watching this train wreck. I can't stand seeing you like this, with *them*," she spits, and I don't miss the hateful tone in her voice.

She turns on her heels and before I can say another word, I watch my best friend walk away. The only person who has stuck with me throughout the years is walking away from me, and there is nothing I can do to stop it.

With my head hung in shame and my heart a bleeding mess I walk back up to my dorm, of course there is a group of girls snickering in the hallway. All three of them give me the stink eye as I pass, but I don't care. I don't know if it's them that massacred my clothes, or Tiffany maybe? Maybe it's even the brothers, I don't know.

All I know is they can cut me with their eyes, and

kill me with their hatefulness but I will still rise the next day, like the sun hanging high in the sky I won't let them stop me from shining.

CHAPTER THIRTEEN

The next morning, I wake up with swollen eyes and a crust sticking to my eyelashes from crying all night. Rubbing the gunk out of my eyes I sit up in bed, for a moment I think my vision is fudged up but then I see that the twin size bed across the room from me is vacant.

I'm alone, Shelby's bed still made, letting me know she never came home last night. Did I lose my best friend? I grab my phone from the nightstand and check to see if she called, or even texted? When I see that she did neither, my heart sinks a little deeper into my stomach.

What is happening to me, to my life? Moving here was supposed to help things, but it seems like it only isolated me, made me weaker, sadder, which is hard to believe since I was sure nothing could destroy me like my father's lies had.

Wrapping my arms around myself I cuddle deeper into Sullivan's sweatshirt, which I'm still shamelessly wearing almost every night. It has long lost the smell of his laundry detergent, but in a weird way it makes me feel closer to him. I should probably burn the damn thing after all he's put me through, but I can't.

It's like a bandage for my heart, a security blanket, because even though I know he's not here and probably never will be again having an article of his clothing makes it seem like he is.

With a heavy heart, I peel the sweatshirt off my body and pull on the last clean pair of jeans I have. I pair it with an old sweater from the bottom drawer of my dresser, while making a mental note to go shopping later and replace everything that was destroyed yesterday.

Going through the motions of my morning routine, I wash my face, brush my teeth, and comb my hair. I don't bother putting on any makeup, since I'm not trying to impress anyone. My eyes catch on the reflection of the person in the mirror. I don't recognize her, the bags under her eyes, and the sadness in her dark gaze. My life wasn't perfect before I came here, but it wasn't this crazy, not this sad. Pulling up my mop of blonde hair into a messy bun, I take one last look in the mirror.

I can do this.

Who cares that someone's after me, or that half the school looks at me like I'm a sasquatch and the other half like they want to hurt me? Or that the three guys I had to fall for are the biggest bullies of them all.

I put my books and notepads into my bag and grab a granola bar to eat on the way to Social Psychology. It's the one class I share with Sullivan and I've been dreading going all week. Of the three brothers, Sullivan has avoided me the most.

Dragging my feet to the class, I make it there just in time. Sullivan is already sitting in his seat, his eyes trained on the professor, as if he can't wait for him to start the class. His arms are folded across his chest, the fabric of his shirt straining, making his arms look even more muscular. Internally I curse myself for even noticing, for thinking about how strong his arms felt when they were wrapped around me, making me feel safe, secure.

There is seriously something wrong with me.

I should not be lusting after one of the men that have made my life hell, after the enemy, the bully. But like a bad habit I just can't kick my addiction to the Bishops. The entire walk to my table I watch him out of the corner of my eye. Sullivan's eyes never move away from the board. He doesn't even glance up at me as I pass him, but I know he can tell I'm there. I don't need him to look at me to know my presence affects him.

I know he can sense when I'm near just like I can do with him and his brothers. I can tell by the way his jaw flexes and his back oh so slightly straightens out, as if he is on edge. If he was a dog, his ears would be perked up right now, listening, and watching for danger.

When I reach my seat, I slump down into it, trying my best to pretend like I'm not affected by him being here. Placing my books, and notebook down on the desk I busy myself, making it look like I'm doing something. The professor starts his lecture, but no matter how much I try and pay attention, I can't.

Like a nervous tick, I spend the entire class chewing on the end of my pencil. I've written some notes down, but to be honest I didn't listen to half of what was said, my mind occupied with the brown haired, blue eyed asshole sitting five seats away from me, the asshole who hasn't even looked my way once. I expected him to be upset about my parents showing up, about the things that they told his brothers, but I never expected him to turn his back on me. I guess if anything I'm disappointed in him, in the fact that out of all three brothers he didn't even hear me out.

Lost in thought, I didn't even realize the professor had dismissed the class until people started getting up to leave. Sullivan is out of his seat and out the door before I even blink, the only proof that he was actually here is his rain water scent wafting through the air. Standing I shake my head in disbelief, how mature. Gathering up my book and notebook I shove them into my backpack and zip the thing before putting it on. Even with all the tension and awkwardness between us I feel a twinge of loss at his absence. I wish I didn't feel this pull towards him, like my heart is breaking when he fails to acknowledge that I exist.

Everything about us is wrong. Wanting to be with them, it's forbidden, like poisoned fruit that's dangling right in front of me. But, they're always slipping through my fingers. I escape the confines of the room and walk out the double doors and onto the sidewalk.

With my backpack slung across my shoulder and my English Literature book under my arm, I start walking towards my next class. I hurry, not wanting to be late for another class. Putting one foot in front of the other, focusing on my steps I don't notice the person approaching me until it's too late.

My lungs deflate and a scream claws up my throat as my backpack is ripped from my shoulder, tugging me backwards with it. My book slips from beneath my arm and tumbles to the concrete.

"What the hell?" I yell, whirling around to face my assailant. When I do, I realize that there are *two* people instead of one, and not just people but men. Fear trickles down my spine. I don't recognize either one of the two guys, but one thing appears in my mind in bright neon, I don't want to know them.

"Why haven't you answered any of our text messages?" One of the guys sneers at me, his eyes menacing in the afternoon sun. It takes me a moment to grasp onto what he's said. First, I think he might just be mistaking me for someone else but then he continues speaking and it's clear that he is talking about the banner with my cell phone number painted on it. "What the fuck? I sent you some nice dick pics, cock, and balls, and I expected you to send me something back."

"Don't you know it's rude not to return the favor? I suppose we can let it slide, but only if you let us see what you've got going on under that sweater," the second guy chimes in, licking his lips like I'm a medium rare steak waiting to be devoured.

"Get lost, douchebags" I spit as I bend down to retrieve my book. *Assholes.* This is just another reason, another thing that proves why I should forget about the brothers. If it wasn't for them, I wouldn't be dealing with this right now.

With the book in my hands I straighten. Mentally I've already made a plan to escape, to get away before this can escalate further, but as I turn to walk away from them, one of the fuckers grabs me, his meaty paw landing on my skin like a hot branding iron.

"Whoa, where the hell do you think you're going? We aren't done here, sugar. I showed you mine and now you're going to show me yours," he leers, his gaze roaming over my chest and even though I'm not showing cleavage, or any real skin, I feel exposed.

"I don't think so," I snap, trying to wretch my arm free from his grasp, but that only encourages him more, and he digs his fingers deeper into my flesh. To make matters worse, the second guy gets a hold of my other arm and before I can stop them, I'm being pulled towards the back of the building.

"Let go of me!" Panic is coating my words. I might as well have not said them at all because they ignore me as if I hadn't said anything..

Panic settles deep in my gut and I'm seconds away from starting to scream at the top of my lungs when a third figure appears beside us. Oh god, and I thought this couldn't get any worse, now there are three of them.

I'll never escape, never be able to fight them off. Inky black dread clouds my mind, and I feel the tears forming in my eyes.

"Usually when a woman says no, she means no." Sullivan growls, the sound of his voice soothing the panic threatening to take over my body. I'm so relieved that I could sink to my knees on the ground to thank him.

"Come on, man, don't be a dick, you can't keep her all to yourself, obviously she likes getting banged by more than one guy, hence you and your brothers using her," he retorts. His chuckles sounding strange.

Sullivan doesn't answer, at least not with words. With superhuman speed he catapults his fist into chuckling asshole's face, shutting both of them up in an instant. The guy staggers back from the hit, releasing my arm as he does.

His friend follows suit and flings my arm away like it's on fire.

"Fucking asshole," the guy moans, holding his hand to his jaw. Blood dribbles down his chin from a cut on his lip.

Momentarily I'm stunned, like a deer in the middle

of the road, two headlights shining on it. The other guy balls his hands into tight fists, and it looks like all three of them might start fighting but then Sullivan takes a threatening step forward, his chest puffed out, his face set in a furious scowl, those massive paws of his clenched into tight fists. He looks like a Viking on the warpath, ready to destroy and kill everything, and anything in his way.

Even though there are two of them and one of him, they cower to him, taking a few steps backwards before turning around to walk away, well, more like run.

I rub at my arms where the skin feels bruised from them gripping it so tightly. Sullivan glares in the direction of the two assholes, before he turns his attention back to me. With a clenched jaw and murder in his blue eyes it looks like he wants to chase them down, to teach them a lesson. Only then do I let what almost happened, what would have happened if he wasn't there sink in. Fear floods my veins, turning the hot blood to icy slush. My whole body starts to shake, my heart threatening to beat out of my chest. A sheen of sweat forms against my brow.

"Has this happened before?" He demands, his hand gripping at the corded muscles of his neck. Tension seeps off of him, and slams into me. I'm terrified, but beneath that fear is something else, anger, sadness, pain, and it pushes through to the surface like a submarine breaking ocean water.

"You mean guys propositioning me? Grabbing me and asking to see me naked? Well yes, actually, see that kind of stuff happens when everybody thinks I'm into it. Wasn't that your plan all along?"

He sighs and looks away, as if he can't look into my

eyes any longer. As if he feels ashamed. I cross my arms over my chest, mentally giving myself a hug. Silence stretches on between us, being this close to him is fucking with my head. I want to kiss him and smack him. Tell him that I did nothing wrong, and make him beg for forgiveness, but before I can do any of those things his sultry voice breaks the silence.

"Oliver isn't coming to English class, so come on, I'll take you there."

Without even looking at me, he starts walking towards the main building. I know he expects me to follow him, but I can't make my feet move. Standing there like I grew roots I watch him walk away. He stops after a few feet when he realizes I'm not following him. I want him to keep walking, but I also want to beg him to turn around, to take me into his arms. I'm conflicted, confused, *broken*.

"Don't be stupid, let's go, I'm not going to do anything to you. I'm just making sure that you make it to the class," he says over his shoulder.

Shaking my head, I say, "I think I've had enough for today. I can't do this right now. I'm going back to the dorms," I tell him, but still my legs won't move forward, it feels like I'm stuck in mud. Not stuck, drowning. All I want to do is go back to my room, lock myself inside, crawl into my bed, and pull my blanket over my head and forget. Forget the brothers, what just happened, the rivalry and all the family drama that comes with it. I want to bury it all, dig a hole and toss it inside.

"Fine, I'll take you there instead." He spins around and starts to walk back towards me, but still I don't move, unless you count my knees knocking together. When he realizes that I don't plan to move he sighs, as if

I'm inconveniencing him.

I don't want to need him, them, but I can't help it. I'm weak, weak for the one thing I shouldn't want, the enemy.

Surprising me further with his actions, he steps closer and snakes an arm around me. Holding me close to his side, he gently starts to guide me back to the dorms. My steps are still unsure but with him by my side, steadying me, my legs seem to do just fine. The walk to the dorms isn't a long one, but today it feels like it's taking forever. Which I don't mind, not when it gives me more time with Sullivan.

Sullivan doesn't say anything, and neither do I. Instead I inhale his intoxicating scent that's wrapping around me like a blanket, sheltering me from the cold. Having him this close after everything that happened, his hands on me, his body close enough for me to feel the heat rippling off of it, it feels like heaven, like a healing balm against a wound. My vision blurs, and big fat tears start to fall from my eyes streaking down my cheeks. Crying is weak, but I'm exhausted, tired of barely holding it together.

We reach the dorms, and Sullivan starts to pull away, but I can't let him, for some strange reason I can't. Turning I wrap, both arms around his middle and press my face into his chest. He feels like him, and as stupid as that is to think I know he's the only thing that makes sense right now.

"Harlow," he whispers, pressing against my shoulders gently. I should have known he would still react with anger, with venomous rage. He peels me off his chest, holding me at arm's length. *He doesn't want you idiot, stop throwing yourself at him.* Let him go.

"I'm... I'm sorry..." I stutter, keeping my eyes on his chest, my head hung in shame so that he can't see how heartbroken I am, how lost I am without him and his brothers.

His hand comes into view, and then he's placing it beneath my chin forcing me to look up at him. With a heavy heart I let our gazes collide. God, he is handsome, like a Greek god, and GQ magazine model had a baby together. That jaw of his is clenched tight, and I itch to trace the sharp contours of his face. The tension in his face seems to ease away, and his gaze softens as he takes in my tear streaked cheeks.

"Do you want to stay here, or do you want to come with me?"

"Come with you?" I question, confused.

"Yes, with me, to the house?" His thumb brushes across my bottom lip. The touch caresses something deep inside me, something primal, and something that's waiting to bloom and break free. I can't explain it, but I feel it.

"You still want me?" How the words manage to slip past my lips I don't know.

Sullivan's blue eyes flicker with heat, "Want isn't exactly the word I would use. We need you, just like you need us. The way you're acting is how Oliver, Banks, and I have been acting since your parents showed up."

"But they hate me," I croak, my throat aching.

Sullivan shakes his head, "Come with me, at least for tonight."

I should say no, walk into my dorm, and go lay down in my bed alone, forever alone, but I can't. Physically, emotionally I can't, and I don't want to. I need them, just as they need me.

"Will you tell them it wasn't me, that I didn't call my parents? Will you help me make them understand?" I ask.

Something swirls in his eyes, and I can't pinpoint the emotion.

"You believe me, right?" The air deflates from my lungs as I wait for his response. I watch his Adam's apple as he swallows.

"Yes, Harlow. I believe you, now let's go. I'll talk to my brothers, get them back on team Harlow." Brushing his arm away I wrap myself around his middle again, holding onto him tightly, just to make sure this is real and not some sick dream.

"You're okay now, everything is okay." Sullivan whispers, a hand smoothing down my back. I squeeze my eyes shut and relish in his words.

It isn't okay, not yet, but it will be soon.

CHAPTER FOURTEEN

I fall asleep on the way to the Bishop residence, my side snuggled into the door of Sullivan's jeep. My eyes blink open as the car comes to a stop. It takes me a moment to realize we've arrived at the house. I'm beyond exhausted, my life is officially falling apart, and all I want to do is crawl under a rock and hide from the entire world. I stare at the monster of a house in front of me through the windshield. I'm worried. Afraid of how Oliver and Banks are going to react when they see me walk through that front door.

"Afraid?" Sullivan asks, as if he could read my mind. I twist around in my seat to face him. He's not smiling, in fact, he looks as cold as a statue. Impassive and cut off from the world. I think on his question. *Am I afraid?* Hell yes. Afraid of losing the last shreds of my heart, afraid of the unknown, afraid of where we will go from here. Is there any hope for us?

"A little," I confess, feeling like all my emotions are on display.

"It will be okay," he murmurs soothingly before

getting out of the car. I open my own door and slip out. The short walk to the front door goes by in a flash. Sullivan twists the knob and walks in with me following closely behind.

I follow him step for step as he walks into the living room, almost as if he is my human shield, protecting me from the wrath of his brothers.

"Hey, what..." Oliver stops mid-sentence when he sees me hiding behind Sullivan. "What the hell is she doing here?"

Banks is sitting beside him, glaring at me, but not saying anything and I have the urge to turn around and run back out the front door.

"Just listen for a minute," Sullivan starts, while Oliver and Banks are already shaking their heads, anger wafting off of them. "She's going to stay here tonight," he announces despite his brothers' obvious disgust.

"Fuck that. There is no way we are letting her stay here," Banks speaks for the first time, his voice as hard as his facial features. "I'm done. I'm done with this whole thing." He declares.

My heart sinks even further. They're going to kick me out. I knew they would, but it still hurts to accept it. I let my head hang low, tucking my chin against my chest, and turn around to leave, but Sullivan stops me, his warm hand gripping my elbow.

"Go upstairs to my room, I'll be right there," he tells me, lifting his chin towards the staircase.

"Are you sure?" I ask, looking up at him, not daring to glance over at his brothers. Their icy gazes are shattering my still beating heart.

"Positive," he assures me. "Go, I'll be right there." He gives me a reassuring smile and call it weakness or a need for attention but against my better judgement I do as he says. I let my feet carry me up the grand staircase.

"This has to stop, Sullivan, we agreed this wasn't going to happen, that you weren't going to..." Oliver's voice drops dangerously low and I block it out, finishing my walk up the stairs. I drag my feet across the carpeted hallway, until I reach Sullivan's room.

Twisting the door knob, I open it and walk inside. I close the door behind me, taking in the space and smell. This strange feeling comes over me, I can't explain what it is, but it feels like peace, like safety, like nothing can get to me when I'm in this room. Slipping off my shoes, I let my body pull me towards the bed. Sinking down onto the mattress I almost moan, the tension seeping right out of me. I press my face into Sullivan's pillows and inhale, his heady scent swirling in my veins. A warmth blankets my body, and for the first time in forever I don't feel alone. I don't feel afraid.

My eyes drift closed, as I slowly breathe in and out, the air passing my lips with ease. I stay like this for a long time, until eventually the exhaustion, fear, and pain of pretending everything is okay overtakes me and I drift off to a blissful sleep, with Sullivan's calming scent surrounding me.

Opening my eyes, I yawn, my gaze sweeping around the room, grey walls, black sheets, it takes me a moment before I realize where I am. The sound of running water coming from the attached bathroom pricks at my ears. I rub my eyes with the back of my hands and look at the door. It's cracked open, steam escaping from the room.

Sitting up on the bed, I run a hand down my chest flattening my now wrinkled sweater. The water shuts off and I hear the shower door open and close. Only then do I realize that Sullivan must be behind that door, and obviously very much naked. My cheeks heat stupidly and my lower belly tingles at the thought.

The door opens, and Sullivan enters the room wearing nothing but a white towel wrapped around his waist. My mouth goes dry and I think my heart actually skips a beat. I don't know where to look first, at his chiseled abs, or his shoulders, or his face, or the delicious V of muscle that leads down to a land that I shouldn't be thinking about. No man should look as good as he does, it's just not fair.

"Hey, you're up. Sorry if I woke you," he says nonchalantly, completely uncaring to the fact that he is not wearing any clothing. Droplets of water cling to his hair, and he shakes it a little bit sending water in every direction.

My chest starts to rise and fall, my nipples hardening against my bra.

"I-I mean, n-no… you didn't… I was…" I stutter, my tongue feeling heavy. I'm flustered even though I'm the one dressed and clearly have nothing to be embarrassed about.

Sullivan starts heading towards the bed, with each of his steps my pulse picks up, thrumming loudly in my ears. I nibble on my bottom lip, trying my best to ignore his presence but it's a lot harder than one would think. I shouldn't be thinking about him like this, naked, wet, our bodies gliding together. By the time he's standing in front of the bed, and only a few feet away from me, my pulse is all but racing.

"You're looking at me like you're scared I might eat you." The grin he gives me could set panties on fire.

"I-I just woke up," I say, mostly because I can't think of anything else to say.

"I noticed," that signature smirk of his widening, as if he knows the power he holds over me. "Do you want to take a shower too?"

"With you?" I ask like an idiot. He smells like soap, and water, and bad choices, really, really bad choices.

"Well, I just took a shower, but I could help you out of your clothes? And with other things, of course." His thick brows wiggle playfully.

Oh my God. He wants to help me out of my clothes. He's basically naked, besides the towel and he wants to get me naked. That would mean we would both be naked. *Together.* I might be inexperienced, but I'm not stupid. I know what happens when people get naked together, and they don't do much talking.

I swallow, but there's no saliva left in my throat, my mouth feels dry like I swallowed a cup of sand. "Okay," I answer meekly, my cheeks burning.

Sullivan blinks, his gaze widening, the playful grin slips off his lips, "You're serious? You want this?"

I lick my lips. Do I want this? Him, and his brothers? Obviously, I want them, but do I want to have sex? Do I want my first time to be with the same boy who took my first kiss, my first orgasm? I shouldn't want it to be him, not after everything, but it feels like I'm whole when we're together and I want to be whole, so badly.

"Yes... I want this... you, I mean... I want you." I stutter out, and grip onto the hem of my shirt, trying to build up the courage to pull the thing off and toss it onto the floor.

With a grin, he moves closer, his movements sleek, smooth, like a cat striding through the night. My body is burning up, it feels like I have a fever. I start to lift my shirt up and pause.

"What about Oliver and Banks?" I ask, needing to clear the air before we take another step. I want them as equally as I want Sullivan, but they don't want me right now, and I need this, the connection to be back in place. I need all of them.

"You want them too, don't you? You want all three of us." There's no judgement in his eyes, no anger. He's simply speaking the truth.

Releasing my lip from between my teeth I say, "Yes, I do."

"And you can have them, all of us, but not tonight. Tonight you're all mine." His voice is low, seductive. Reaching for me, he brushes some lingering strands of hair from my face, the simple touch sending my already stimulated nerve endings into overdrive.

I consider telling him that I'm a virgin but decide against it. What if he changes his mind because of it? I don't want to ruin the moment. I'm given little time to dwell on the thought before Sullivan pounces on me. The towel around his waist slips to the floor, and I gasp, just as he takes my cheeks into his hands. He kisses me, gently, but with an underlying hunger that has me eager for more. He kisses me until I'm breathless, until my chest is heaving, and my hands are shaking, until my lips are swollen. Until there is nothing but the two of us.

He only stops kissing me long enough to help me out of my clothes. Dipping his fingers into the waistband of my jeans, he drags them down my legs along with my panties, leaving me bare to him. Slinging them over his shoulder, they land on the floor somewhere behind him. My bra is next to go. He reaches around me and with skillful fingers he is somehow able to undo the clasp. My breasts fall forward without the support of my bra.

With a devilish grin that I feel deep down to my toes he flings the contraption over his shoulder just like he did the rest of my clothing. Then there's silence as he takes a moment and just looks at me and I do the same in return.

His pupils are dilated, his eyes seem black instead of their normal stormy blue. His chest rises and falls rapidly, and his jaw is set in a hard line. He looks ruggedly handsome. My eyes wander lower, past his well-defined stomach and down the trail of russet brown hair leading me straight to his very erect penis. I gulp, I've seen dicks before, but nothing could prepare me for one *that* size entering me.

"Scared?" Sullivan asks smugly, stroking the thing leisurely, like he has all the time in the world.

"No." I shake my head, lying while trying to hide the nervousness from my voice. "I've just never..."

"Been with a guy as big as me?"

Arrogant asshole.

"Yeah, you could say that."

"I'll go easy on you, Princess." His wink makes me smile shyly, I can't help it. I have no idea what the hell I'm doing here. "But first..." He leans over me, his body hovering above mine as he lowers his head to my breast. His hot, wet tongue drags over my swollen nipple before he closes his mouth around the tight peak and starts to suck.

Sweet baby Jesus.

I moan into the room, my hands roaming over

Sullivan's toned back and shoulders, pulling him even closer. Unable to lie still, my body moves like a snake underneath his touch, wiggling restlessly, my back arching off the bed. My body begs for more, it needs more.

He cups my other breast with his warm hand, kneading it, then he starts rolling my nipple between his thumb and index finger just as Banks had done. The sensations spiraling through me are explosive.

"Lie back," he orders gruffly, and I follow his command without thought or hesitation, coming to rest against his soft sheets. "So fucking pretty," he murmurs, nudging my legs apart. I can feel his eyes on my flesh. "I'm going to taste you, so be a good girl and stay nice and still. I need you soaked with need before my cock comes anywhere near your pretty pussy."

I swallow around the lump of fear forming in my throat and nod my head, my hands fisting into the sheets as he situates himself on his belly, spreading my legs wider to accommodate his huge form between my thighs.

He lowers his head, bringing his mouth to my center. I can feel his hot breath on my already slick folds, and I shiver at the onslaught of sensations rippling through me. I'm barely grasping onto reality, hanging on by a thread and then I feel his tongue dragging across my most sensitive parts. It's a brief touch, a caress, the feeling so foreign, so intense, I can barely handle it. No one has ever done this to me, no one's ever touched me this way and all I can think is that I want more, need more. Like an addict I'm desperate, willing to sell my soul for my next hit.

My hands leave the sheets and find their way into his thick silky-smooth hair. Threading my fingers through the strands, I rake my nails over his scalp. He releases a throaty moan, the sound vibrating through my core, coaxing a moan past my own lips.

"Ahhhh..."

"You taste exactly like I knew you would. Like strawberries and cream," his skillful tongue swipes over the sensitive bundle of nerves and my hips lift, a jolt of pleasure rippling up my spine.

"Sullivan," I whine, wanting more of him, feeling this deep, primal need trying to escape out of me.

"Patience." He tsks, with a light chuckle before getting back to work on tasting me. Using his fingers to spread my folds and suck on my swollen clit. The need builds, starting from behind my eyes and through every inch of my body, out of reflex I squeeze my thighs together, but Sullivan doesn't care, he continues to lick and suck as I grow slicker and slicker, my arousal damn near pouring out of me.

When I'm positive things cannot possibly get any better, he slips a finger into my channel, while still keeping pressure against my clit. He pumps in and out of me a few times, before adding a second finger and stretching me deliciously. Thrashing against the pillows, I bite onto my fist to stop myself from screaming out loud as he fingers me, while sucking on my clit with unforgiving need.

A blinding light flashes before my eyes, and my hips rise and fall as an indescribable pleasure lays claim to my soul. Sullivan's thrusts slow, as I slide down the mountain of pleasure.

"Oh my god," I whimper when the last ripples of pleasure have run through my body. Sullivan chuckles against the sensitive flesh of my thigh, his breath tickling me.

I don't even want to know how good sex will feel if it feels this amazing and all he did was use his fingers and tongue.

Before I can catch my breath, he starts kissing that same patch of skin and continues moving upwards, peppering open mouth kisses over my thighs, belly, ribs, and all the way back up to my breasts.

By the time he gets to my collarbone I can feel his enormous erection pressing up against my leg, his smooth skin caressing mine as he moves his body between my thighs. I'm panting now, salivating.

He reaches over to the nightstand and opens the drawer, digging around inside it. The break of passion gives me a moment of clarity. What the hell is he doing? A second later he pulls his hand out of the drawer, a small foil package in his hand.

Condom. *Oh shit, I almost forgot.* Looking down at me with raw need he rips the silver square open with his teeth. Taking the condom out, he reaches between us with one hand. Part of me wants to take a peek and watch him put it on, but I don't think I can actually tear my eyes away from his. It's like we are tethered to each other, an invisible hold binding us.

With his hand still between us, I feel him guiding himself to my center, and I spread my legs even further for him. The smooth head bumps against my still sensitive clit and my thighs automatically squeeze together at the sensation.

"Relax," he whispers into my ear as he starts to rub the head of his cock up and down, through my folds, spreading my juices over his cock before he brings himself back to my entrance.

Holding himself up with one arm his lower body

against mine, his hips press into mine like a missing puzzle piece, the head of his cock pressing against my entrance. With a gentleness I didn't know he could possess he enters me slowly, stretching my walls, making me take all of his thickness.

He lowers his head, nestling his face into the crook of my neck, and I am glad he does, because I don't know if I could hide the tiny surge of panic and discomfort I'm experiencing right now. Needing to touch him, I grip onto his biceps, my nails sinking into the flesh leaving small half-moon indents behind.

I feel full, so full, and I know he's only inside a few inches. I gasp as a small sting and a slight burn ripples through my core as his cock breaks through the resistance, taking my virginity. I've given him all my firsts, and my heart. Sullivan must not even notice it, because he just keeps pushing inside of me until there is nowhere else to go, the head of his cock bumping against the back of my channel.

His lower body is now completely pressed to mine, leaving no space between us. With minimal effort he hitches my leg up, and swivels his hips, pressing deeper inside me. My chest heaves up and down, my heart fluttering so hard I'm sure even he can hear it.

"Fuck, this is a tight fit." Sullivan blows out a heated breath, sweat beading his brow, and I wonder if he's ever done *it* like this.

Seated deep inside me, he lifts his head his eyes moving from where were connected to look up at me. I can tell by the tension in his muscles that he's restraining himself. His lips part, and his gaze darkens.

"Do you want me to fuck you hard and fast or slow and gentle?" The edge to his voice, and crudeness of his words scares me a little, but I remind myself that this is Sullivan.

My Sullivan.

"Slow, please," I answer with a strong voice. With a clenched jaw he pulls all the way out of me, the air rips from my lungs with the sensation, and before I can fill them again, he's entering me, slowly, so slowly.

"Do you wish it was all three of us doing this with you right now? That we got to take turns with you? Making you come over and over again."

"Yes," I answer breathlessly. "I would like that," I admit shamelessly. Sullivan smiles, his eyes lighting up, as he continues his slow leisurely strokes. Pulling out and pushing back in. In and out. In and out. Eventually the dull ache gives way to red hot pleasure that spreads out through my abdomen like lava erupting down the side of a volcano.

"I always knew it would be this good." Sullivan grunts, and he looks so beautiful right now, his eyes closed, his body straining above mine. I want to remember this moment for the rest of my life, the one singular moment in history when a Lockwood and a Bishop became one. Because that's what this is history and we're going to rewrite it.

"I've got to speed it up, Princess," Sullivan pants, his hot minty breath fanning against my throbbing pulse. "This slow pace is killing me."

"Okay," I give him a little nod and turn, pressing a kiss to his mouth. I drag my tongue across his bottom lip, silently asking for entry.

He opens for me all the way and our tongues meet for a sensual dance while he starts thrusting inside of me, his hips piston upward, going deeper, harder, and faster.

His cock rubs against something deep inside me, and I feel the pressure building in my womb. He breaks our kiss and stares down at me, a wealth of knowledge and secrets in his gaze.

"I want you to tell me when you're close," Sullivan orders, and I nod unable to form a cohesive word.

He changes positions then, pulling away and pressing back onto his knees. He grabs onto my hips pulling me into him and in this position he seems even deeper, like he's a part of me.

My lips part into the shape of an O. And each time he bottoms out inside me a sliver of pleasure ripples through me. With a feral grin Sullivan places his thumb against my overly sensitive bundle of nerves and with all the sensations overtaking me it doesn't take long for me to reach my peak.

"I'm-I'm...coming," I gasp, barely getting the words out before my thighs start to quiver and my toes curl. My back arches off the bed, and Sullivan starts to curse as he holds me in place my pussy squeezing his cock with an evil vengeance.

"Fuck me," his pace grows faster, his grip on my hips harder, his head tipping back as euphoric pleasure overtakes his body. And then I feel his cock pulsing inside me as he lets out a deep animalistic growl before slamming into me one last time.

He collapses on top of me with a huff, his sweat covered body, blanketing mine with warmth and safety. I relish in this moment, having him so close, where no hate, no parents, no drama can reach us. I know the moment can't last forever, but I can hold onto it, keep it close to my heart. He rolls off me a second later, falling to the mattress beside me.

He reaches down and pulls the condom off with a wince, before throwing it into the trash bin next to the bed. I look down at my thighs, hoping that I didn't bleed onto the sheets.

Not wanting him to stop touching me, I roll over with him, planting my head on his chest and draping my arm over his torso. I close my eyes and suck in a deep breath. With my ear right above his heart, I can hear the steady rhythm clearly, like my own personal lullaby.

As if the sound was just made for me, calming and soothing me, I'm lulled to a deep slumber and for the first time in a long time I'm falling asleep knowing that everything is going to be okay now.

Everything will be fine, as long as I have Sullivan.

CHAPTER FIFTEEN

"This feels nice," I whisper into Sullivan's skin the next morning. Taking a deep breath, relishing in his scent, I run my fingers over his stomach, tracing each muscle as I go. I've been up for ten minutes, which I spent every second of cuddling and touching Sullivan.

He only woke up about five minutes ago and I'm not sure if it's because of all my touching and teasing or if he is just having morning wood but his cock is hard as steel. A sizable tent forming between his legs. My head would like to repeat what we did yesterday, but the dull ache between my legs says otherwise. So instead of instigating sex, I simply keep running my fingers over his skin.

"Yes, it does feel nice. I wish it was real," he says almost absentmindedly.

I smile at his words. "Of course this is real, why would you think anything else?" I ask, without looking up.

"I know this isn't real for you. I know you don't actually want me." My hand on his stomach stills. Confused I raise my head so I can see his face. I take in his somber expression wondering why he is suddenly in this mood.

Still smiling, I ask, "If this isn't real for me and I didn't like you then why would I have given you all my firsts?"

"All your firsts?"

"Yes," I admit. "I gave you my first kiss, you gave me my first orgasm, and last night I gave you my virginity."

"Stop, Harlow," he growls, suddenly pushing me off of him. My mouth pops open and I'm completely dumbfounded by his sudden mood change. "I know...I know this is all a game to you. Do you really think I would believe you? Believe that I was your first kiss? That you were a virgin?" He tips his head, back and chuckles, "I might be stupid, but I know a liar when I see one, and you, Harlow Lockwood, have and always will be one."

I'm so stunned by this whole situation, that I'm literally speechless. He shakes his head and pushes off the bed. Stomping to his dresser, he pulls out the drawer with such force it almost comes out all the way. He grabs a pair of shorts from within and puts them on, damn near ripping them in the process.

"Sullivan, I'm not lying, last nig..." I say, once I find my voice again. Why does it feel like we're falling apart?

"You deserve an Oscar, you know?" He cuts me off, whirling around with a coldness in his gaze. "Your acting skills are on point. Maybe you'll start your acting career with the video I took of us fucking last night."

The air stills in my lungs, the only sound I hear is the thump, thump of my heart. It feels like it's being ripped in two and at any given second I expect it to stop working. His confession destroys me and shatters my world.

"You... you... filmed us having sex?" I stutter, my hands shaking, tears forming in my eyes instantly.

A smile spreads across his face and even though it seems forced, it wounds me deeply. Disgust and hurt spread through my body and I can't stop it. I scurry off the bed and gather my clothes from the floor, putting each piece on as I go. I can't do this anymore. I can't keep being their punching bag, reliving a past that I'm so helplessly trying to break free from.

With everything but my jeans on I glance over at Sullivan who just stands there watching me with an unreadable expression.

"You're right, I *am* a great actress. So committed to my role, I grew back my hymen for you, to make this more believable," I spit out, shoving my legs into my pants, I point to my thighs which still have streaks of blood on them. Sullivan follows my gaze, his mouth pops open when he sees the small smudges of blood. "Don't believe me asshole, check the condom, or maybe think back to the way you fucked me, of how nervous I was," I pull my pants up the rest of the way and button them.

Sullivan looks like he's about to say something, but I'm done. I'm not waiting around to hear what it is he has to say. Some lame-ass apology that means nothing. Because I mean nothing to him. To them. I'm so done. Done with the lies. Done with the games. Done with him and his brothers, his family, all of it. Just done!

"Have a nice life," I murmur on the way out of his bedroom door. Tears escape my eyes as I run through the house.

"Wait," I hear Sullivan call from upstairs just before I slam the front door behind me.

How could I have been so stupid? I gave myself to him. I loved him, I loved all three of them and all they did was play games. I'm nothing more than a pawn to him and his brothers.

I run down the sidewalk, my shoes pounding on the pavement, and the tears running down my face uncontrollably. Pushing my legs as far as I can, I only slow when I become lightheaded. Needing to catch my breath after running through the neighborhood for I don't know how long. My chest aches, my lungs burn, and a killer headache has formed right behind my eyes.

I stop and look around, taking in my surroundings, and I realize that I have no idea where I am. Reaching into my back pocket I pull out my phone and find the contact info for the only person I can think of right now.

Caroline answers after the third ring. "Harlow, what's up?" Her voice is cheery, as usual. Completely oblivious to my despair.

"Caroline," I sigh with relief, "can you come and pick me up?"

"Of course, are you okay?" She loses her cheery tone, concern replacing it.

"Yes, no, god, I don't know. I'm at…" I look around me, trying to find a street sign. "McKinley Road," I say when I finally find one.

"I'll be there in ten minutes."

Ending the call, I sit down on the curb and let my head fall into my hands. I vow to myself never to be dumb enough to fall for their tricks or antics again. By the time Caroline's car pulls up, there must be a puddle of tears in front of me, because I haven't stopped crying since I got off the phone with her. She jumps out of the car and runs around to where I'm sitting.

"Oh my god, what happened?" She kneels down next to me, her arms circle around me. "Please, tell me. What's wrong?"

"It was all a lie... Sullivan and his brothers played me," I say in between sobs. "I loved them and..."

"Oh, Harlow, I'm so fucking sorry. Come on, girl, let's get you home."

"No, I don't want to go home. I need to talk to Shelby. Can you take me to the gallery downtown?"

I need to apologize to my friend, she warned me about the Bishops, and I didn't listen. She's been the only constant in my life, the only one who always stood by me. She is the only one I can trust, and I've been neglecting her. I need her, now more than ever.

"Of course, come on," she ushers me into the passenger seat, and even buckles me up when I don't move to do so myself.

"Are you going to tell me what happened?" Caroline asks halfway through town.

"I...I don't even know. Everything was fine one minute and then it wasn't." Which is the truth. One minute it was pure bliss and the next, utter horror.

She doesn't ask me any more questions and I'm more than grateful for the silence. I don't think I could answer any more of her questions anyway.

"Thank you, Caroline," I gaze over at her once we've stopped in front of the art gallery. "I mean it, thank you. You've been a great friend."

"Any time, Harlow. Call me if you need anything." We hug before I exit the car. My face is still red, and my eyes are still swollen from crying but I'm past being self-conscious.

Taking a deep breath, I push the gallery's doors open, a bell rings above my head and I walk into the clean space. Modern looking sculptures are sitting on hip high pedestals in the center of the space and pictures of all sizes are decorating every wall in the room.

A petite woman walks into the showroom greeting me with a wide smile. She is wearing a skin tight pencil skirt, a matching crop top, and four-inch high heels that look like they could break some ankles.

"Hi, can I help you?"

"Yeah, I'm looking for Shelby. I'm sorry to show up here, I know she is working but this is kind of an emergency."

"Who?" The woman looks genuinely confused, her eyebrows drawing together.

"Shelby," I say louder, she must have not heard me clearly.

"Doesn't ring a bell. Is she one of our artists?"

"Oh...ah, maybe... maybe, I'm at the wrong gallery, I'm sorry," I say embarrassed, before turning on my heels.

"This is the only gallery in town, miss."

I freeze with my hand hovering inches away from the doorknob. My mind goes blank and then this feeling of utter dread creeps its way up my spine and settles into the base of my skull.

Nothing makes sense, everything I thought I knew is wrong. My life built with building blocks of lies and deceit and like a Jenga tower someone pulled the one piece that has it all crashing down.

I feel like I'm trapped in this moment, my mind frozen in time. My thoughts hovering somewhere in between disbelief and unbelievable despair.

"Are you okay, miss?"

No... no, I'm not okay and I don't know if I ever will be.

I walk back outside and down the sidewalk. I know there are people walking down the side of the road like me, cars driving on the road, I know they are there, but

I don't see them clearly. Everything around me is a blur. My mind overwhelmed with everything that has happened today.

My body's numb, my emotions in disarray. I feel like I'm not even here, like I'm only a shadow of myself, a ghost who isn't part of the world at all.

Putting one foot in front of the other, at least I think that's what I'm doing. I look up, the scenery changing around me, the ground beneath me suddenly seems different. Sounds piercing through the fog surrounding my brain. Someone is screaming, but I can't make out what is being said. Then something catches my eye. I look up to see two bright lights heading straight for me. But I'm not fast enough, there is no time...

◆ ◆ ◆

Darkness.

Nothing but darkness.

I'm not sure where I am. But wherever it is all I know is darkness. This place has no end, no beginning, no up, down, right or wrong.

There is no love or hate, no pain, but also no happiness.

I try to remember how I got here, or where I'm from but my mind is nothing but a wasteland.

All I am and all I know is darkness.

Until one day, when there was more.

Beep.

Beep.

Beep.

A steady rhythm calling me from somewhere unknown. The sound seems close and a million miles away all at once. For a long time, that's all there is.

"It's been ten days," a woman's voice suddenly breaks through.

"Mrs. Lockwood, these things take time. Harlow suffered a major brain injury. It will take time for her to recover. I can assure you that she is in the very best hands here at the clinic."

"She better be, considering what we are paying you," another man's voices meets my ears. It's deep, scary even and I make a mental note not to mess with that man.

After that, I hear the opening and closing of a door, followed by chairs moving around.

"You heard the man, love, let's go home, there is nothing we can do for her right now."

Suddenly, I have the overwhelming urge to open my eyes, I want them to see that I'm here, that I'm awake. I don't want to be left alone in the darkness again. Willing my eyes to open, it takes every ounce of strength I have. I feel like my eyelids have turned into lead and my strength has diminished to one percent.

Still, by some miracle my eyes slowly blink open. The bright yellow light coming from the ceiling overhead blinding me momentarily, but I keep squinting and blinking until I can make out the room and its contents.

"Oh my God! She's waking up!" The woman's high pitch voice hurts my ears a little but her hands covering mine are soft and warm and make up for the pain. "Oh, Harlow, you're okay. Everything is going to be fine now, I promise."

I blink, confused, then I look down at her hand and

pull mine out of her grasp.

    I look up into her big tear-filled blue eyes, horror, and shock reflect back at me and I ask the only question that I can, "Who are you?"

To be Continued...

Next in this Series

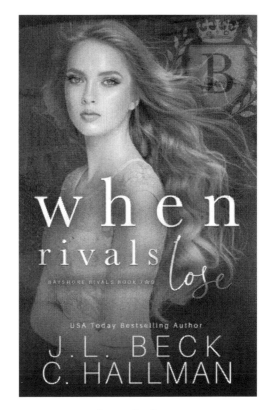

When Rivals Lose

Other books by the Authors
Each book is in Kindle Unlimited

Their Captive (Dark Reverse Harem Romance)

The North Woods University Series

The Bet
The Dare
The Secret
The Vow

The Rossi Crime Family Series

Convict Me
Protect Me
Keep Me
Guard Me
Tame Me
Remember Me